THIS IS NOT A LOVE SONG

DARK LOVE STORIES

SEAN O'LEARY

Touching Base published in *Spillwords*

Fremantle published in *Quadrant*

Norseman published in *Quadrant*

Pawn published in *FourW*

And whatever happened
To Tuesday and so slow?
Going down the old mine with a
Transistor radio
Standing in the sunlight laughing
Hiding 'hind a rainbow's wall
Slipping and sliding
All along the waterfall with you...
Van Morrison "Brown Eyed Girl"

CONTENTS

TOUCHING BASE

I met an Aboriginal guy in Kings Cross. I'd just finished an all-nighter shift in a dodgy motel on Darlinghurst Rd. It was summer and we sat in the gutter. I gave him a cigarette and he said to me:

'When my father died I cried so much that I had no tears left. Acid burned out of my eyes, into my skin.'

I looked at his face, there was scar tissue in the tracks of his tears. That's serious sadness but strangely it made me feel better.

'How long ago was that?' I asked him.

'About ten years, but I still feel sad.'

I told him how I was over the job. Over Kings Cross and he said, 'You have to go then. Move. Do something else,' and he started laughing, said, 'I'm not sad all the time and you don't want to sit in the gutter the rest of your life.'

And I could see he was ok, making a joke of life.

It made me realise that life post-schizo diagnosis wasn't so bad. I'd been in love a few times. I might have friends if I cared to dig them out. I smoked another cigarette with him but he didn't say anymore. I went home and slept for ten hours, and when I woke up I woke, I staged a mini-revolt in my life and quit the shitty job. Caught the bus to Melbourne.

———

I'm at the Homeground office in East St Kilda. I don't need crisis accommodation, just a clean boarding house for a month or so until I can get some work, reconnect with a few people.

I should ring Sarina who has tried to be a great friend over the years. I should still be on good terms with her except I didn't return her calls. She tried many times to get in contact with me, but I was, I don't know, not well. What about Ryan? An old and true friend, same story. If I told him I'm holed up in a boarding house in St Kilda, the reaction would be:

'Oh shit! What happened? A boarding house?'

Like I might have committed a crime, done something awful to have ended up like this. Best wait until I've got some work, a flat, organised, decent.

The thing about going crazy, being psychotic is when you get better, get back to a level of normalcy. Your confidence is so shot you find it difficult to get out and about. Forget about it when you're psychotic. That's bloody scary stuff. Voices and feeling threatened and thank God I don't have to put up with that anymore. (Please God.) Good old medication. Hmmm. I had the diagnosis though. Chronic schizophrenia, and it was the chronic that worried me.

The boarding house was clean. A lumpy single bed, desk, bar fridge and wardrobe but so dark. Even in the middle of the day. No light unless you leave the door open and then you have no privacy. Smoke outside so you can breathe when you're inside. The room is like a child's bedroom without the good stuff.

I've applied for five different jobs. One night porter job; one-night packer job; three call centre jobs. Should keep Centrelink happy and hopefully put me in work. It's not the work I could do, but I can't go back to that other high-stress life.

I'm smiling a little more lately. At least that's what I'm telling myself this morning. I don't think the other tenants like me. Paranoid or truth? You tell me, I don't fucking know. I don't sit around in tracksuit pants and shoot the breeze with them. One guy told me to eat at the Sacred Heart Mission to save money. How I am supposed to react to that? Yeah. Cool. That's about a forty-dollar saving or I'm not that destitute and fucked up so please stay away from me.

I look normal. If you saw me in the street you wouldn't think, that guy's a schizo who lives in a boarding house. They see me, the other tenants, looking neatly attired and say, 'He's up himself.' But I buy all my clothes second-hand at Vinnies and other Op-shops. They drink alcohol; I don't. Or maybe they just roll their eyes and say, 'Get fucked,' under their breath. I'm a little lacking; I know I am. In confidence and interpretation of what the hell is going on in my head. Shaky ground. Not fitting in anywhere; not accepted. Hence the night-shift jobs. No one to fit in with. I'm in a rut after five weeks in Melbourne, and what happened to that smile I had ten minutes ago? Give yourself a break, man, it's only been five weeks.

Hard questions to answer when you're out of sorts, a little nervous and with still some lingering bad thought processes and paranoia. Push yourself, Nicky. I make an appointment to see a psychologist (free with Medicare) in the city, in a building in Flinders Lane.

The psychologist's name was Colin. He was dressed in jeans, a white shirt, and a sports jacket even though it's hot. He has that look nailed. Perhaps he might need some patches on the elbows of his jacket; yes, some cord patches and he could star in the sequel to *The Dead Poets Society*. But I'm being facetious and he wants to help. Get some volunteer work into you, he suggests. I tried that but they wouldn't have me. He gives me a strange look and packs me off and out the door.

I wake up the next morning, my thoughts are not in order. I know straight away it's going to be a bad day. I rush to get out of the boarding house with my thoughts racing to Fitzroy St, order coffee (stupid?) at the bakery, cinnamon donuts, three. I walk to the beach fast, breathing hard. You have to talk to someone. Do it. I go to a phone box and call Sarina, now slightly calmer. I tell the truth for ten minutes, gush it all out decrying embarrassment, and she gives me what I want. We agree to meet the next day at 11 am, Saturday. I feel great, my smile is back.

We agreed to meet at the State Library, Swanston St. I walked around, found a spot in the shade, hope I don't seem too wired. Too overtly happy to see her, but why shouldn't I be? I don't see her until she gently touches my back with her hand and pecks me on the cheek.

A little smile from me.

'Hey, Nick,' she says. 'You look good, you've lost a little weight but good. Still smoking, I see.'

'Sarina, yeah, you look good too, as always. Can we sit down together somewhere?'

'What about that bench over there?' she says, and, 'Let me get a coffee first. I'm so hungover. Nothing's changed.'

She rushes off. I sit down looking at the trees and thinking green—calm because my heart and thoughts are racing along superfast.

We were never together, just friends.

'Ah, thank God,' she says, holding up the coffee, almost

worshipping it. She plays with her bracelet, pushes her hair back behind her ears, says, 'Nick, I know you haven't been well, even before the call yesterday. How could I not know? You've had a bad time.'

I feel a little sad and put out that she thinks I'm somehow totally fucked up, but I push the thought aside. *She came to see you.* I pull myself together out of the 'feeling sorry' state and say, 'Have you seen Ryan?'

She doesn't say anything for a minute, seems to age right before my eyes. Tears roll down her cheeks.

'You're not the only one who fucked up, Nick. Ryan killed himself about a year ago. Don't you take that bloody option.'

'Look, Sarina, if he felt like I did at my worst, there may not have been an option. Was it...'

'Don't you bloody get it, Nick? Ryan and I were together. You can't tell me anything I haven't seen before.'

I don't know what to do with my hands or how to make things right, and she leans into me and puts her head on my shoulder. We sit like that for ages until she says, 'Thanks for turning up, you prick. You bloody well let me down that, many times, I nearly gave up on you.'

'Yeah, well, here I am. A shell of a man.' And I laugh at myself.

'You're ok, Nick.'

'Am I?'

'I always liked you, you know.'

I get nervous again.

What happens now?

SEPARATING

It was always just us, ever since we met at Renton in year six. Renton was this co-ed private school we all went to in Melbourne. We used to meet at the train station before and after school. Natasha and Molly were friends already. They had started at Renton in year four. Mike and I had become friends because we were the two new kids at school in year six. Then one day, as these things happen, we just started somehow talking to Natasha and Molly on the platform of Glen Iris station. Kids from about five or six different schools all met there, to smoke to delay as long as possible getting to school. Not that we were smoking, yet. Anyhow, that's how we met. I wish I had a better story about it but I don't. We're all graduated. Oh, graduated is so American I shouldn't use it. We finished year twelve three years ago. We're happy, but everything between us changed quickly and that's what I'm going to tell you about.

It's 1 AM, I go to the counter and order four coffees, three hamburgers with the lot, and a souvlaki. The souvlaki is for Molly; she loves that meat cut straight off the rotisserie, shoved into a pocket of pita bread, covered in lashes of white garlic sauce. There's not too much you can say about the hamburgers except they are huge at The Diner on Swan St, Richmond, in Melbourne.

The Diner tries to be like those diners you see in American movies; a front counter with stools running along it, booths running along the wall opposite, above them, pictures of famous boxers and movie stars. Only there's no endless cup of coffee like you see in those movies, you know, where the old tired wisecracking waitress asks our hero if he wants a refill. Anyhow, this is July in 2013, we've been meeting here since we connected properly on the station that day. I'm with Natasha; Mike is with Molly. It was a big deal when we were younger, maybe fourteen or fifteen. We'd come here on a Saturday after-noon, order coffee, smoke cigarettes. We felt like adults. Now, we usually finish up here at the end of the night. But our nights aren't crazy drinking nights powered by drugs. We stayed in, mostly, at the house where Mike and I lived in Mary St, Richmond.

We smoked a little dope and drank a few beers, but what got us going was trying to create stuff. I was trying to be a writer and Natasha acted in and made short films and studied at the College of the Arts. I worked at 7-11 to get cash and Natasha was lucky that her parents still gave her money, and she had this great little apartment above Horton's Books, near the corner of Gertrude and Smith streets, Collingwood. Mike was into painting and visual arts and worked at the National Gallery on St Kilda Road as a part-time guide. It suited him. He had so much knowledge and liked to impart it without being a big head. Molly was a gun photographer. She had already been part of an exhibition, along with other upcoming painters and photographers at a gallery on Smith St. Some of her photos had sold and it was in this environment, at the share house, that we operated so to speak. Oh, and my name is Dom, and Molly worked part-time for a wedding photographer.

Molly was the most independent of the four of us, often leaving the three of us at the house in Mary St while she went off wandering around taking her photos and coming back hours later looking pleased with herself and saying, 'I got some good shots; I'm really happy.' She liked the area around Carlton Gardens, Royal Exhibition Building, and the Melbourne Museum.

We pretty much ditched all the others from Renton the second we walked out of the school gates for the last time, and they didn't care about us, except we somehow pissed them off by being this tight foursome of friends. We certainly didn't care about them. I guess the big thing was they didn't invite us to their parties, which were supposed to be a big deal. So whenever I met anyone I'd been to school with, and Melbourne isn't that big when you're that age, I never knew what to say, because I hadn't been to Mac's party or Andrea's party the night before. And they always asked me, what is it that you four do? and I never gave a straight answer to that question.

Mike and Natasha got up to play pool in the backroom after they had finished eating. They always ate as if their lives depended on it. Molly took small bites and chewed slowly like the souvlaki was going to be the last one she ever ate.

She stopped eating for a second and said, 'What are we doing, Dom?'

'You mean after this?'

'No, I mean with our lives.'

'I thought we were pretty good. We're all doing alright, aren't we?'

'Don't you think it's odd? Just the four of us all the time.' She stands up and fidgets in the pocket of her coat. Pulls out a packet of tissues. She looks quite beautiful in her long blue woollen coat. She's wearing black jeans underneath it and her hands are barely visible as the sleeves of the coat are too long, and she smiles at me and I smile back and she says, 'Sometimes I think you and I know each other from before; we've indeed known each other for a long time and from a youngish age, but I can look at you and know what you're thinking, and I know you can do the same with me.'

'I know what you're talking about. I get it with Natasha too but not on the same level.'

'I'm the same with Mike. Think we should do something about it.' She sees me get embarrassed but keeps staring at me. I don't say anything, and she says, 'C'mon Dom, let's spice things up.'

And then she starts laughing and I say, 'Well, I didn't know that was coming, so maybe your theory's all wrong.'

'Come out with me tomorrow. I'll pick you up at Mary St. I'm staying at my parents' place tonight. I'll borrow my brother's car. Alright?'

'Fine but what...'

'It's our secret, Dom. I'm going out taking photos and I want you to come.'

'OK. What time?'

'Ten sharp.'

'OK, ten *sharp* it is.'

This guy dressed in black jeans and a black leather jacket with a blue open-neck shirt walks in. He's tall and handsome with thick dark hair, and I recognise him as Sammy Jackson, one year behind us at Renton but he's a big boy now. I'm surprised when he comes straight over to us.

'Hi, Mike, hi Molly. Seen Natasha?'

He's with a very young-looking blond girl with a pixie haircut, wearing an olive-coloured dress with a fur-lined black jacket over the top. I have to admit it's a rock star entrance and it has kind of flummoxed me that he's asked for Natasha. I try and be cool and adjust how I'm sitting in the seat, but it doesn't help that I look like crap wearing old track pants and a hoodie to keep out the cold because my house is only ten-minutes away.

I say, 'Out the back playing pool.' Sammy looks at Molly but she ignores him and starts eating that souvlaki again. He goes out the back and I want to ask Molly why he's asking for Natasha, but I don't, and he comes back five minutes later and smiles at us as he walks out, the young blond sexy girl flowing along behind him.

Natasha and Mike come back a few minutes later and I say, 'What did Sammy-the-rock-star want with you?'

Natasha looks pleased that I'm so curious, some jealousy in my voice. 'I ran into him today on Smith St and I said we might be here, that's all.'

'So, he turns up here for five minutes just to see you.'

'Yeah, and I bought some speed from him.'

'You're taking speed now?' I ask.

She looks at me and says, 'There's a party tomorrow night at this huge house in South Yarra on Punt Rd and Sammy invited us all.'

I'm wondering where all this is coming from. I make a mental note to remind me that Molly totally ignored Sammy. I say, 'And the speed is for the party.'

'Yes, for all of us.'

'Not for me,' Molly says.

Nobody says anything for a few minutes, and then Natasha says to me, 'Can we go home to my place?' She has that look in her eye, like, I want to bonk your brains out, so I nod and say goodbye to Molly and it's like she said. She knows to pick me up in Collingwood in the morning.

We catch a taxi back to Natasha's place in silence, and I'm

glad not to be talking about Sammy and speed. At her apartment, she turns the heater on and takes off her jacket and jumper. Sits on the little ledge under the window facing Smith St, some light from the streetlamp catches her face. She hardly ever wears make-up. She has long rope-like brown hair and wide-set dark brown eyes. She smiles at me, and I sit down next to her. She lights a cigarette and I kiss her and her tongue pushes into my mouth and we kiss deeply for a few minutes until she breaks away. She keeps smoking as I kiss her neck. She stands up and takes my hand and leads me to the bed. Butts the cigarette in an ashtray on the chest of drawers. We stand next to the bed kissing, and I run my hands over her bum as she drops back onto the bed, bouncing a little and laughing, taking off her t-shirt and bra.

Natasha and I both wake up early, if you call nine early. I get out of bed and go to her wardrobe where I keep some clothes, put on blue jeans and a dark blue t-shirt, throw my black hoodie back on. I connect Natasha's iPod to some small speakers and turn it on low volume, and it's Jagwar Ma with 'The Throw' and she says, 'Thank God you put something decent on.'

'It's your music.'

'Figures.'

'I'm going out with Molly today to watch her take her pictures.'

She nods like it's nothing out of the ordinary, and I think about something Mike once said to me. He said, 'If you ever had the inclination, you could screw whoever you liked, and if someone told Natasha, she simply wouldn't believe it. She trusts you implicitly.' And at that moment I wish she didn't.

I stare out the window across the street to Dr Java and I say, 'Want a coffee? I'm going across the road to Dr Java.'

'Yes, please,' she says, and I look at her and she has this shit-eating grin on her face.

I ask, 'Why so happy?'

'I always like you best in the morning after we've had great sex the night before. Come over here.'

I stay where I am and she says, 'What are you doing way over there, lover?'

'Don't call me that. I bloody hate it. If I get into bed, you're going to want to start something and I told you I'm going out with Molly.'

'Dear old Molly and Dom-the-good-guy. What a pair.'

'What'd you mean exactly?' I ask, but she doesn't say anything just turns over and manages to, accidentally on purpose, show me her bare white arse, which is rather nice, but I walk out and down the stairs and across the road to Dr Java where the coffee is always good.

Back upstairs Natasha gets out of bed naked and walks right in front of the window on her way to the bathroom, so if you were staring into space on the 86 tram bored out of your brain you might have got a nice surprise. I hear her turn the shower on. I finish my coffee and ten minutes later, finally covered up with a towel, she walks over to her cupboard to choose the day's outfit. Yes, it's a small studio, kind of a ware-house-style flat but bigger than you think given my description of the goings-on. My cell phone goes off. Molly.

'Hi, are you ready?'

'Not coming up?'

'No, I don't want to pay for parking. Come on. It's a freezing cold Melbourne winter's day. What are you waiting for?'

She cuts the line.

Natasha looks at me and says, 'Have fun with your new girlfriend.'

I think *screw you* but don't say anything, just walk out.

Molly said she was borrowing her brother's car. I'm not sure what kind of car it is, and then I hear her blasting the horn diagonally across from me on Smith St, about fifty feet back from Gertrude St, and people in their cars and on the street are looking at her and I bolt across the road. It's a new Volkswagen Beetle, sky blue, and she has the door open for me.

I say as I get in, 'Love the car, but aren't we just going up the road to Carlton?'

'Not today. Today it's the beach.'

'Which beach?'

'It's a surprise.'

She does a U-turn and goes back down Smith and turns left and drives down to Punt Road, so I figure we're going to St Kilda Beach. I don't even mind when it starts raining and I say, 'I'm hugely in favour of rain and winter in general.'

'Me too. I have a huge umbrella if we get caught out.'

'What's Mike up to?' I ask.

'I don't know,' she says and she kind of twists up her face. And then she says, 'Dom, I think there's going to be a lot of change going on soon, and if you're not prepared you might totally lose it.'

What a weird thing to say, I think, and she does that reading-my-mind-thing and says, 'Think about last night. The rock star. We meet people from Renton by accident, Dom; they don't come looking for us. At least they don't come looking for me.'

I don't say anything until a few moments pass because it's not a conversation I want to have if she means what I think she means, so I ask, 'Why do you like Carlton Gardens and the Royal Exhibition Building so much?'

'Actually, truly, my thing is those two huge steel structures outside of the Melbourne Museum. I don't know why, it's like they're some kind of airport runway to the skies. Or like huge freeway flyovers except they're beautiful to look at. People must think I'm crazy when I look at them and take photos because I walk backwards underneath them, looking straight up while filming them with my cell phone and taking still shots at the same time. But I don't care what people think; they just get to me and that's what good architecture is, isn't it, if something moves you like that.'

'Thanks for the speech, but I can't see what's so great about them. I never took much notice of them and I'm always walking through there from Natasha's to Carlton, to go out for coffee or go to Readings or something.'

'Well, take the time to stop and admire them on your next little walk. Don't just bustle along; look up and see the wonder.' And we both start laughing. We're on Fitzroy St now, but she doesn't look to park; she continues to Jacka Boulevard, past Donavon's Restaurant and St Kilda Beach onto Marine Parade, away from the city. She smiles but I don't know where we're headed, and the rain starts coming down heavier.

Molly has red hair and freckles that start on her left cheek and run across the bridge of her nose to her right cheek. Her hair is a bit of a bird's nest. I think she's beautiful, whereas Mike always says to me he loves her even though she's plain-looking. She's confident with her body too but doesn't wear tight or revealing clothes like Natasha does, or if she does it's once in a blue moon, so when you see her it takes your breath away. Takes *my* breath away. Those shining dark blue eyes too, it makes her special. Mike's crazy.

We park in a side street off Beach Rd in Mentone. The rain is soft now. She takes the umbrella, but we don't use it. She says, 'I want some shots of the deserted beach and birds swooping down onto the ocean, and back up again and later maybe the cliffs at Beaumaris or Black Rock. OK?'

'Anything's OK. I'm just along for the ride.' We take our shoes off and walk down a cement path to the beach and down across the coarse cold sand to the water's edge, and I say, 'Sandringham Beach has the best sand; nice and white and not rough like this is.'

'Let's walk back towards the city and then turn back and walk to Mordialloc Pier.'

We walk slowly without talking and she takes her photos of the beach and birds, large and small, flying and swooping about and the rain stays away, and I like the look of intensity she has when she takes the photos. We reach the Beaumaris cliff face and turn and walk up to the path, which is about thirty metres from the water, and walk back towards Mordialloc that way. We stop at this stone shelter that has a wooden roof; it's like a bus stop on the beach.

She says to me, 'Do you remember when we were twelve or thirteen and we played kick to kick at Chadstone Park?

'Yeah, of course.'

'You were always there early, practising your shots at goal on your own. Looking so serious. Natasha and I would walk towards you from Chadstone Road and you'd turn around to line up your kick again but you'd see us, and even though we were two hundred metres away I could see the smile on your face. I always thought you were looking straight at me, and whenever I think about it now, it makes me feel good. Mike hated us joining in because our kicks fell short and we were always talking but you didn't care; you just kept playing.'

I don't know what to say and we walk back down to the water's edge again and begin the walk to Mordialloc Pier.

'Do you think this is special, this part of Melbourne?' she asks me.

'I think it's underrated. People always compare Melbourne's beaches to Sydney but that's crazy. You have bay versus surf and this is a different kind of beauty. It's sparse here. From Bondi to Maroubra it is chock full of people and cafés and pubs. Of course, there are people here and pubs and cafés too but not with the same density as Sydney, but I don't hang around here much. It is kind of desolate even though we're only thirty minutes drive from the city and in a built-up suburban area, but that's because it's winter and the weather is shit to most people.'

'I started coming here at the beginning of winter and kept coming back,' she says, and we keep walking and she hands me the umbrella while she takes some shots of what I think are little egrets and also these large white birds with long wingspans. Neither of us knows what they're called. She takes a few more shots kneeling, looking back from the way we came. There's no-one else on the beach, not even someone walking a dog. The wind has died down but it's still cold.

She gets up and spontaneously hugs me and I laugh and she says, 'How's your writing going?'

'Nice, at least I think it is. I had another story accepted, this time by *Sapphire*.'

She looks at me while shaking her head and says, 'Dom, you should be telling everyone about this. *Sapphire*. That's huge. Have you even told Natasha?'

'No, she gets weird when I get published. It's only been twice before but she seems like she almost hates it. Hates me doing well.'

We start walking again and she says, 'Things are changing, *speed*. I'm just hoping you get it, Dom.'

We climb up on the pier and there are three hardy souls fishing, their legs dangling over the side. Out of nowhere three girls dressed in long black bike-pants and Lycra tops run onto the pier and all around us and then leave as quickly as they came.

'Molly, what was that?' I ask.

'I think they belong in Brighton,' she says, but I don't get it and we keep walking out to the end of the pier and the wind picks up but I like it, getting buffeted about out here facing the horizon.

Molly leans into me and I put both my arms around her and say, 'This is allowed, isn't it, between old friends?'

My cell phone goes off. Natasha.

'Hello.'

'Where are you?'

'Mordialloc.'

'Where?'

'St Kilda. We're walking along just near the Sea Baths.'

'Why?'

'Molly's taking photos.'

'Are you coming to the party in South Yarra? I want to get there around ten. We can go for a drink somewhere beforehand.'

'Just come to the house in Mary St.'

'OK, but I want to go out. I have that stuff from Sammy.'

'I can hardly hear you,' I say. 'I'll be home in a couple of hours.'

'Hey! Wait! Is Molly coming to the party?' I look at Molly who shakes her head at me and I tell Natasha no and press end call.

We stay on the end of the pier until Molly says,

'There's a café on the walking path at Parkdale. Feel like a coffee?'

'Yeah, will it be open?'

'Probably.'

Molly pulls up out the front of my house in Mary St, Richmond, and I ask her in but she shakes her head. I'm getting out of the car and she says, 'I'll be at home all night, Dom.'

I close the door and she drives off. Many years later I look back on this day, those few hours with Molly, and it always makes me feel warm and good about life. What she said about the kick to kick. It meant a lot to me.

Mike is lying on the old dilapidated couch smoking and I say, 'Hi.'

He looks up and says, 'Didn't Molly come in?'

'No, she said to tell you she'll be at home all night.'

'Natasha said you went taking photos with her in St Kilda.'

'Um, yeah.'

'Are you coming to the party? I think I'll take some of the speed. Once can't do you any harm.'

'Party, yes. Speed, no.'

Natasha arrives at Mary St around eight, and she has her hair piled up on her head and wearing black tights and boots with a tight-fitting black jacket. She looks kick-ass fine. Mike is into this eighties music phase that is wearing a little thin with me but Natasha seems to like it and I hear INXS singing 'The Devil Inside' for the fiftieth time this week. She takes the little plastic bag filled with white powder out of her purse and lays it on the table and says, 'Shall we?'

Mike kneels on the carpet next to the table with Natasha who empties a little pile and starts dividing up the powder into lines with her credit card and doing it like she's done it before, which doesn't impress me. She snorts up a line through a fifty-dollar note, hands the note to Mike who does the same. Hands me the note and I say, 'No.'

'Oh, come on, Dom. Loosen up. It can't harm you,' Natasha says.

'It's some mysterious white powder cooked up in a back-yard drug kitchen most likely by career criminals who are clearly concerned about quality control. No thanks.'

She groans loudly, and we all agree to leave and go to the Great Britain Hotel where we are supposed to be meeting Sammy Jackson and others. I don't feel good about it and Mike says to me, 'Hey, this stuff is really working. I feel great.'

'I'm happy for you.'

The Great Britain is a short walk away, and as soon as we walk in, Natasha lets her hair down. Let the games begin. Radiohead is playing and I see the rock star and his little blond girlfriend straight away. They're surrounded by their friends and I recognise a few people from Renton. Everyone seems to know Natasha and I wonder how this is possible; I think about what Molly was saying to me all day about change. Radiohead suddenly gets louder and Mike looks a little on the outside like me until the blond starts talking to him. I try and get in among the group but I can't seem to start a conversation with anyone. Natasha has her arm around Sammy Jackson, laughing and flirting, and so it goes on for the next hour or so. Natasha and the blond girl, who I find out is Nicki Furlow, head off to the bathroom several times together and Mike is now the life of the party. They're all up, the whole group, and Natasha is embarrassing me with her full-on infatuation with Sammy. We leave at ten and the party is in a huge mansion on the top of Punt Road.

There is what you could only call a huge ballroom just past the entrance hall to the house, house, which is incredibly ostentatious but quite superb. Natasha is hanging all over me and gushing about how handsome I am to try and make up for her behaviour in the pub but it just pisses me off. She's grinding her teeth a little bit and drinking vodka and lime out of a can. Sammy enters the ballroom, and she backs off me a little bit, though still being attentive. Mike is way off in a corner dancing with Nicki Furlow and looking like he's the king of the world. I break away from Natasha and make my way outside. Natasha follows me and we find a spot under some fairy lights in a big old tree.

'Isn't this party out of the world,' she says. 'The house, that ballroom, it's like it's from another age, all these people. I want to keep doing stuff like this all the time. I wish you'd loosen up, Dom. People are wondering who you are?'

'You mean they're wondering why I'm with you or more perhaps why *you're* with *me*.'

'Oh, I can't deal with you, Dom. I'm going back inside.'

And I let her go. I call Molly and tell her I'm coming over. I walk out of the huge gates onto Punt Road and walk down to Toorak Rd and hail a taxi and ride to a block of flats in Carnegie. Molly is sitting out the front on the small brick wall, in the same jacket and jeans she was wearing today.

I sit down next to her and I say, 'Yes, indeed, you saw it coming.'

'We're alright if it's just the two of us, Dom,' she says. 'I've been waiting for you to come around. I thought you'd never get it. Mike and Natasha need something bigger. Let them have it.'

ALICE

His shift was dawdling along. Even the two American sailors on shore leave were having a quiet night. No hookers arriving by taxi and looking wonderfully salacious in the lift just before the door closed. A couple of nights ago one of these hookers had been so beautiful that it took his breath away. It was summer. The end of February. Warm rain fell down in the night outside the small motel in Potts Point.

Then Alice walked into the reception area, wet from the rain and looking lost. She stared at him her eyes red-rimmed from drugs or crying or both but blue like the sea at Bondi. She wore a black bra under her red t-shirt, Nadan could see the outline of her breasts.

She said rapidly, 'I need some help. I'm in trouble. I don't have any money until tomorrow. I can pay you back tomorrow. Just give me a room for the night, please. I'm not a prostitute.'

Here we go, Nadan thought, but he looked at her again. She was skinny and her short, dirty-blond hair soaking wet, and yeah, she was crying. She wore the skinniest skinny jeans in the history of the world and black thongs on her feet. She carried a large brown bag, like an oversized handbag.

It was 10PM. Nadan finished his shift in two hours. The girl, Alice, stood looking at him and he said, 'If I give you a room, I lose my job.'

'That's your excuse.'

'What did you say?'

'Nothing. I didn't say anything, come on, please, don't you have an old dirty used room I could use?'

Nadan did have such a room, but the guy who worked the midnight shift, he was sort of crazy efficient and he checked all the dirty rooms each night. He was Chinese, this guy. Smoked cigarette after cigarette standing outside the reception door all night but did his work and was fearless when there was trouble. His name was Chen and he told Nadan it meant great in Chinese; Nadan wanted to say, what's so great about working the graveyard shift in a motel in Potts Point. Nadan was a Croatian name.

Alice sat down on a wicker chair and Nadan looked at her as she closed her eyes and mouthed the word, *please*. He thought through his options quickly and said, 'You can use a room for an hour if you like. Take a shower, clean up a bit, but that's it.'

She smiled and said, 'You're a good person. I knew you were a good person.'

'I have to check your bag.'

'What. Why?'

'I can't have you shooting up in the room. If you screwed up and OD'd, well, the police and...'

'I'm on methadone.'

'The bag.'

She thrust it at him as he walked from behind the reception desk. The bag contained three pairs of underwear: white, blue and black, all lacy. A blue singlet top and a black t-shirt. A purse, a packet of Alpine cigarettes, a red lighter and a pair of black jeans. Lots of medicine in pop packs. And she had mace. Nadan wondered if she'd used it before.

'You feel like a coffee?' he asked her.

'Oh, yes, please, but I want to have a shower first. I'm so wet, my t-shirt and jeans and...'

'I'll take you up, and remember, only one hour.'

'I appreciate it, I really do,' she said, speaking really fast again.

He let her in the room and said, 'Dial 9 when you finish your shower and I'll come up and we can have a coffee.'

'What about your desk job?'

'I'll forward the switchboard to my cell phone and lock up. I do it all the time. Are you feeling better?'

'Yeah, but what happens to me after an hour?'

'I don't know,' Nadan said and closed the door.

So, after she rang him, he knocked on the door and Alice opened it. He said, 'Hey, I didn't ask your name.'

'All friendly now, huh.'

'You just say whatever you like don't you, even though I'm helping you.'

'It's Alice.' And she turned the kettle on and said, 'There's no coffee sachets.'

'I have some. One or two sachets.'

'Two, no, three,' she said, 'and four sugars. And oh, you brought real milk, good.'

He made the coffee and his cell phone rang, 'Cosmopolitan Motel, Nadan speaking.' He listened and then said, 'No, I'm sorry, we're booked out tonight.'

'Are you really?' Alice asked as he closed his cell phone.

'No, but I'm having coffee, we can smoke in here too. One of only three smoking rooms, we were lucky.'

'You're a real conscientious guy, aren't you? Can't give me a room because you'd lose your job and you leave your post and smoke cigarettes and have coffee and tell people the hotel is full when it isn't.'

'And I give a room to a young woman on methadone who may or may not be a *working girl*.'

'I won't answer to that. I'm trying to get my life back to... back somewhere.'

'You're pretty young,' he said, taking a sip of his coffee and blowing smoke skywards, 'so you've got plenty of time to fix it, and how old *are you*, Alice?'

'Twenty-one.'

'I'm twenty-three.'

'What kind of name is Nadan?'

'A good one.'

Neither of them says anything for a while, and Nadan stubs out his cigarette and says, 'I have to get back.'

And just as he's about to close the door behind him, she says, 'Don't work too hard.' And he smiles and shakes his head.

Time moves slowly, and at 11.10PM Nadan calls Alice in the room and says, 'Hey, I'm sorry, but my replacement, Chen, he's a hard-core guy who, unlike me, takes his job seriously and...'

'I'm coming down now.'

The lift door opens and she steps out looking a whole lot better than she did an hour ago.

He says, 'What now? Will you try the same shit somewhere else?'

'If I wasn't desperate I'd teach you some manners. Just because I'm in this...oh, forget it!' She walks straight out the door onto Macleay Street and turns left up towards the hazy neon lights of Kings Cross, and Nadan feels like a complete tool. Just for a second, he thinks about chasing after her but he shrugs and thinks, not my problem.

Chen arrives at ten minutes to midnight, and Nadan thanks him for being early again. He hoped Alice hadn't left anything incriminating behind.

Nadan walks up Macleay Street and turns right onto Darlinghurst Road, passes the Bourbon and Beefsteak Bar and the Aussie Rules Club and then cuts across the road past the tiny Astoria Hotel and passes a café. He sees Alice sitting on a stool facing Darlinghurst Road, a cup of coffee in front of her and he can't help himself, he smiles. She sees him and rolls her eyes and then looks down. He walks along the street further towards the station, she might have smiled, he thinks, but, oh yeah, what an arsehole, she probably thought.

Then he spun around and went back inside and sat next to her and said, 'Do you want another coffee, my shout?'

'Can I have a pot of tea?'

'Sure. What kind?'

'Camomile and what about a toasted sandwich,' she asked in a small whiny voice.

Nadan shook his head and said, 'Sorry, I don't get paid until tomorrow but I can get the tea.'

'Thanks.'

They sit not saying very much, and on Mondays there is only one more train to Bondi Junction at 12.35 AM and Nadan tells Alice he really has to go now.

'OK.'

'Are you just gonna sit here all night?' he asks.

'Probably, although that manager guy at the counter might kick me out or...'

'Listen, you know what. I think you're OK. You can stay at my place tonight. Don't worry, there's a couch you can use. I'm not hitting on you, just don't steal any of my stuff.'

'Something tells me you don't have anything worth stealing.'

'One minute you're begging for a room, then I do you another favour by...ah, and now you're all sassy again.'

Nadan is of medium height and slim but not skinny. He's been eating a lot of shit food lately, so he's started getting a very small gut which he doesn't like much. He has black hair and dark brown serious eyes and full lips for a guy. He parts his thick black hair down the middle like John Travolta did in *Saturday Night Fever* because it's one of his favourite films even though he wasn't born when it opened. *(We could be dancing, yeah!)*

Nadan decides he'll spend his last $12 on a taxi home and he says to Alice, 'Did you ever go to Barons?'

'What is it?'

'It was this really cool club/nightclub. It had rich, red velvet chairs and cushions on the floor. There was no dress code and it had these heavy drapes and it was open all night and people played chess and backgammon, and I never remember there being any fights there. It was across the road there (and he points) down Roslyn St.'

'And you miss it?'

'Yeah, my sister's older friends took me there when I was seventeen and to the Piccolo Bar and Bar Coluzzi during the day in Victoria Street. I was like a kind of mascot or something but Barons made the biggest impression.'

'What's there now?'

'I really don't know. I heard it was some big, huge, run-of-the-mill nightclub but I never bothered even looking.'

Later, they sit together in the back seat of the taxi and he asks her, 'Has it been tough on the methadone?'

'Yeah, but it's more than that. It's the whole cycle of scoring and the people I know. I had to leave all my friends behind because they...'

'Because they're all junkies, huh?'

'Yes. You don't have many nice things to say do you?'

'You don't talk like a junkie.'

'Thank you, Professor Higgins.'

'Who? Oh, you mean like in that old movie. The girl who couldn't...'

'Talk proper.'

'Yeah. But look, I'm confused, how come you're in Kings Cross if you're trying to get away from these people.'

'They all live in Erskineville and Newtown and around there, not Kings bloody Cross, that's where they score and live or sometimes we'd score in Marrickville.'

'The Marrickville Mauler.'

'What?'

'Jeff Fenech. Australia's greatest ever boxer.'

'Oh right. And you know what, getting away from those people was hard. I'm still trying every day not to go back.'

'So really, you're pretty brave for leaving them behind.'

'I guess.

'How long have you been on methadone?'

'Six weeks, six weeks I haven't had anything but methadone.'

'Good for you,' he says, 'come on, we're here.'

Nadan lives on Hall Street about five hundred metres up from Campbell Parade, next to a café. She follows him up one flight of stairs and they walk to the end of the balcony; he opens the door, turns the light on and lets her pass.

She says, 'Oh, it's a studio apartment.'

'What'd you expect, three bedrooms and oh, there's your bed,' he says pointing to the couch. There's a big window, the blinds are open and you can see Dover Heights and there's lots of sparkling lights from the houses and flats.

She says, 'At least you have a nice view. All those little

lights look like stars. What's that big Mexican hat doing on the wall?'

'I dunno. I bought it in one of those $2 shops. I thought I'd wear it to the beach but I never did.'

The double bed is in the middle of the back wall of the studio, and in front of it is an average size TV and a DVD player. There are bookshelves full of books and DVDs and Alice says, 'Wow, look at all the movies and books.'

'Yeah, it's the one thing I don't do, sell my books and DVDs and...'

'I don't get it. Why would you sell...are you, do you take drugs?'

'I smoke a little pot. I have some if it will make life easier for you. Better than shooting up,' he says and notices her arms and says, 'You don't have any track marks on your arms.'

'I mostly snorted or injected it into my toe and only sometimes in my arm and there were some tracks but they cleared up. Do you think I should have them as reminders?'

'No, er, I dunno. I'll roll a joint. You can choose a movie if you want. I'm pretty tired. I have headphones you can use. You can watch one while I sleep.'

'I might sleep too, after that joint.'

In the morning Nadan wakes up at 10 AM with a hard-on and sits up and rubs his eyes and Alice blurs into his vision. She's looking at him and wearing the headphones; she moved the TV to in front of the couch. He tries to adjust his dick in his briefs but gives up and grabs some fresh undies out of the top drawer of his chest of drawers and makes a run to the shower. There is a pair of jeans on the floor of the bathroom and he puts them on after he gets out of the shower and walks bare-chested to stand next to the couch. Alice looks up at him and he looks at the TV screen. She's watching *Big Wednesday* and it's the scene where Jan Michael Vincent is drunk and William Katt kicks him off the beach.

'Good choice,' he says to her. She holds her hands out and mimes, *can't hear,* and he shakes his head and goes into the kitchen and makes coffee for both of them. When he brings her cup out, she smiles and he places it in her hand and sits beside her on the couch. She takes the headphones off, goes to the TV and pulls the jack out. The sound booms out and they sit and watch it together to the end. He stands up and digs his right hand into his jeans pocket and finds a ten-dollar bill and laughs to himself. He never did that before or not in a long time.

'I have the day off,' he tells her. 'I always get payday off and I volunteer at the Salvation Army in Bondi Junction. My pay doesn't go into my account until 1PM.'

She shrugs and he says, 'I feel weird leaving you here, but, um, here take this ten dollars. I'm going to be out most of the day.'

'Wow, thanks.'

'When do you get your dole money?'

'Three days.' Nadan remembers her saying at the motel she'd have the money today.

'Hmmm. Um, I'll be off then. Are you feeling OK, not hanging out for a hit or anything?'

'No. I have to go to a chemist in the city to get my methadone. I just feel...I dunno. It's nothing. Don't worry, go out, have fun.'

'Alright, bye. Oh, hang on.' And he goes to the chest of drawers and scrapes all the change off it and puts it in his pocket and takes a key as well and gives it to her and says, 'I guess you can stay another day if you want.'

'Oh, thank you, thank you,' she says, and Nadan smiles and nods and leaves.

Alice watches him leave and decides she's going to follow him. She waits for two or three minutes and then walks quickly out to Hall Street. She follows him to the newsagent where he buys a newspaper. He crosses Campbell Parade and waits at the bus stop. She waits about fifty metres away and the 380 bus arrives quickly, already near-filled with people. She sees him find a seat near the front. She gets in the back door while people exit the bus and the driver doesn't see her or he couldn't be bothered pulling her up and they ride to Bondi Junction.

He gets out the front door and she exits the back door. He walks for a couple of blocks and then goes in the front door of the Salvation Army and she watches him from behind the doorway. He doesn't go into the kitchen or talk to the Salvos in uniform. He nods at a few different people and he gets a tray and joins the food queue. A woman puts a hot meal on his tray and he smiles and thanks her and goes and sits down and eats and he has the paper open reading. He's not bloody volunteering, he's eating there. Alice *cannot* believe it. What on earth is going on? Afterwards, she follows him back to where the bus dropped them off and he sits on a bench seat checking his watch all the time. Waiting for 1PM, she thinks, and then he goes to an ATM and then into the TAB and she sees him going from form guide to form guide underneath headings of Brisbane, Port Augusta, Warracknabeal, Taree, Bunbury, Flemington, Rosehill. He's a gambler who eats at the Salvation Army. She's not the only junkie addict.

Alice starts to hurt a bit, physically and mentally. Her situation is only marginally better than yesterday. But she has a roof over her head for another night or two. She can't get a flat. The bond would be two dole payments and they want four weeks rent in advance too. She doesn't want to get payday loans yet; they probably wouldn't lend her anything anyway or not enough. She tried a couple of boarding houses around Darlinghurst but they were full of men. Desperate men who hadn't worked for years. She runs her hand through her short hair. *I need to wash it*, she thinks. Fuck. 'I just want to get away,' she mumbles to herself, or did she think it? Must be going nuts.

Her plan is to get the next dole payment and then head down the south coast to Nowra or somewhere, rent a caravan near the ocean. Forget everything that has ever happened to her. She walks to the station and buys a ticket. She has enough money left for a cheap pack of cigarettes. There was half a loaf of bread in Nadan's fridge. She could make toast. Was there margarine and milk? She couldn't remember.

She goes to the chemist on George St, and the chemist in charge tells her to come around the counter and he hands her the little cup and she drinks and he says kindly, 'Everything OK with you? You look nice today.'

'I'm OK, thanks.' She walks out. It is starting to get hot. She goes to a tobacconist and buys a packet of cheap Chinese cigarettes, but when she turns around, he's standing right behind her, Neville. Her heart starts beating really fast. She looks down, away, anywhere but at him.

'Hi, Alice,' he says.

'Hi, I'm in a hurry. I have to go now.'

'I'll see you soon. I know where you get your methadone now,' he says, and she can't believe he just let her go like that. She hurries back to Town Hall Station. She sold herself to Neville one night for the price of a deal. She did a lot of stuff in that share house she wants to forget about; can't forget about. She'll definitely go down the coast now; can't be running into people like Neville. A new doctor and chemist in Nowra, yeah, a new everything.

At Bondi Junction she waits across the street watching

Nadan again and she sees him walk out. She follows him again and he goes to a block of flats on Denison Street and walks into the lift and disappears. She goes in and watches to see which floor the lift stops on. Floor 3. The lift comes back down and she gets in and presses 3. Not really sure why it matters to her what he does. But he was good to her. Didn't try anything on her. Made her coffee in the morning. She gets out and walks along the corridor. There's what looks like an office at the end of the corridor, and she walks in and she sees prices for different types of massages. She worked in a place like this once, desperate for money, and it wasn't so bad. There was no sex and finishing them off by hand was nothing. Not at the time but she thought about later and it confused her. She got sacked for always calling in sick and being late. She asks the receptionist if a guy wearing blue jeans and a black t-shirt with thick dark hair came in and she says,

'You his girlfriend?'

'Yeah, but don't tell him I came in. I'm not mad at him.'

She looks at Alice like she's crazy and says, 'Whatever.'

And Alice leaves and walks all the way to Hall Street and uses the key to get into the flat. There is margarine, which seems like a huge victory and milk she hadn't seen and coffee and she has cigarettes and a bed for another night. Heaven.

Nadan comes home at 5PM and Alice has just started watching the news on channel 10 and she says, 'Do you want a coffee, I'm about to make one.'

He looks tired but he smiles and says, 'Yeah, that would be great. I'm going to call for a pizza around six. Anything you don't like on pizza.'

'I can't really think, but...um, do you mind. Can you afford it?' she asks, thinking of seeing him in the Salvation Army, eating.

'I had a small bet today and I won a trifecta, nothing huge but it was a good win.'

'How much did you win?'

'All up, hmm, about four hundred.'

'Whoa! Do you gamble much?'

'No.'

'Because I saw you eating in the Salvation Army today.'

Nadan looks at her like he's going to kill her.

A beat. Two beats.

'You followed me?'

'I'm sorry. Look, it's OK. I don't care. Everybody has their problems, please, I...'

'You are some fucking piece of work! I let you stay here. I give you money and a key to my flat and you fucking follow me!'

She looks away from him and then goes into the small kitchenette and she turns to look at him and he looks like he's going to boil over and she says, 'I'm sorry. I really am, but I like you. You've been kind.'

He turns and goes into the bathroom and stays there for five minutes where he splashes his face with water a few times and breathes heavily in and out. When he comes out he says, 'Fuck it's hot in here.' He turns on two fans that he has and closes the blinds. 'Fuck! I wish I had an air-con.' Then he goes into the kitchen and puts his hand on the back of Alice's neck and squeezes her neck gently and says, 'Don't worry about it, Ok. You've got enough problems. I like vegetarian pizza. I'll get the biggest size they have and a huge bottle of Coke and we'll smoke a joint or two.'

And Alice turns around and looks at his dark brown eyes and says, 'Thanks, Nadan,' and she rests her head down on his shoulder.

He puts his hands on her shoulders and holds her at bay and says, 'It's cool, those fans work pretty good actually.'

They're eating the pizza on his couch and watching this old Western called *Shane*, starring Alan Ladd and Van Heflin with Jack Palance as the bad guy. When Alice asked him what it was about he said, 'A stranger rides into town and...' And he stopped talking and said, 'Best watch it without any idea of what's going to happen.' Now three-quarters of the way through, she has laughed and cried and almost cheered during a fight scene.

He rolls a joint and they pass it back and forth between them. The film ends and Alice is crying, and Nadan says, 'Pretty good, huh?'

'Yeah, yes, it was brilliant. If I saw this movie in a video shop, I wouldn't even think about borrowing it with that cover it has and being so old and I hate westerns but that little boy and the father and...anyway you know all that.'

'I might lie down,' Nadan says, 'I'm pretty stoned.'

'Can I lie down next to you?'

'Um, I guess, sure.'

And they lie down on the bed and Alice says,

'You have a gambling problem, don't you?'

Nadan's about to hit the roof again but he checks himself and says, 'Like you, I'm trying to get better. I...I can't help it. I get so wild in those TABs and pubs, drinking coffee or beer and smoking like a chimney and watching race after race, all my wages riding on horse after horse. It can be so thrilling and so... sometimes I come home just exhausted.'

'What would your sister think?'

'My sister is dead, and you know what, I have a job and I pay rent.'

'Whoop-de-do. And I bet you're way behind in the rent too.'

'Not way behind. A couple of weeks that's all.'

'How did your sister die?'

'A hit and run. The guy who did it was a junkie; fucking high on smack. He didn't know what the fuck he was doing and my sister's dead.'

Alice feels the force of what he just said and waits a few beats before talking quickly again, 'Oh, Nadan, I'm sorry. That's insufferable. Life is so shit sometimes. I'm going to go down the south coast when I get my next payment.'

'Insufferable. It fucking was. Is. And you're the most well-spoken junkie, er, ex-junkie in the history of the world.'

'Did we go over this before?'

'Yes, sorry.'

'Right, so yeah, south coast. Good idea, huh?'

'And do what?'

'Rent a caravan close to the sea. Forget about everything that happened before the day I move in. Stay clean. Be a good person,' she says and rolls over and wraps her arm around his waist, spooning.

He presses some weight back against her and says, 'Sounds like a plan.'

'I saw this guy today,' she say,s her hand drifting down over his fly, 'and I don't want to see him or any of those people again.' And she undoes the button on his jeans and says, 'I like you, Nadan.'

An hour-and-a-half later he says, 'That was great. It blew my mind.'

'Thanks so much.'

'I'm tired though.'

'Me too. Are you sure you don't want me to move to the couch?'

'Of course not.'

'Of course.' *Oh, fuck,* Nadan thinks, *just be quiet now.* Everything was so good.

They both sleep late and Nadan has a shower and gets dressed for work in his black suit pants and white shirt. He doesn't have to wear a tie to work. She looks at him and he says, 'Worst part about the job, wearing these shit waiter clothes. I'm not a bloody waiter.'

'Not much better...forget it. Sorry.'

He looks at her and says, 'I start at twelve today. I'll call you later on. Oh, you don't have a phone. Here,' he says, 'take mine. I don't have anyone calling me anyway. Bit of a lone wolf.'

'Me too, now,' Alice says.

'I'll call you from work.'

On the bus, Nadan thinks about what it would be like to go with her to the south coast. Be like her. Forget about the past; his sister. His mum and dad had died a few years ago, both within a few weeks of one another. Nothing to keep him here. *Stop gambling,* he thinks half-an-hour later as he walks into the TAB in the Crest Hotel Arcade in Kings Cross. It's a quarter to twelve. He lied about starting work at twelve, he has three hours gambling time and $600 in his pocket.

He goes to Randwick Race 1. Ah, his favourite jockey, long-shot Jamie Innes and on a 30-1 shot. He starts big (for him). $50 to win. It comes third. Each-way never entered his mind. He has a few $10 bets on other long shots and comes up with nothing. He goes to Melbourne racing, puts $40 to win on a 20-1 shot and comes up short again. Already the anxiety has increased and, of course, what he's doing is madness and he knows it. Backing long shots, but the adrenaline rush when they get close, when the jockey pulls the horse out wide in the straight and sets the whip cracking and never quite makes it, not yet. Nadan likes the rush and, like he said to Alice, he drinks coffee and chain smokes just outside the TAB door, looking in like a little boy lost. Even if the 20-1 shot won, he'd only get $800. He started with $600 for God's sake. And on and on he goes for a couple of hours and he starts to get nervous. Another week of eating at the Salvos and smoking Champion Ruby.

He takes a short break. A walk down the dirty half-mile and back. He smiles and shakes his head at the girls who proposition him and glares at the drug dealers. He knows it so well but has no love for it. It is a soulless place full of misery and people lost and others just trying to obliterate themselves either for a weekend or the rest of what may be short lives. He's back to the Crest Arcade and his luck is out. He's down to his last $100. He puts on two box trifectas, one for the last race at Randwick and one for a harness race at 9PM. Last chance saloon.

Alice makes her way into the city again for her methadone and tells the friendly chemist she won't be back, she's moving to Gosford, she lies to him just in case Neville or any of the others from the house in Erskineville try to find her. She's not hurting so much. Sex last night helped. Nadan was quite good. Nice strong body and telling her he wanted to exercise, get rid of his gut. Guys were just as worried about how they looked as girls. And it was real. She liked him. He liked her but she was leaving tomorrow. Too many temptations in the city, but she knew drugs found people. Didn't matter where you went. Other users saw it in you, wanted to drag you in. Even small places had drug dealers. The whole world had a drug problem she thought.

Nadan checked in a young couple from Brisbane in their early twenties, full of life, asking all sorts of questions about nightclubs and good pubs, where to get the best pizza. They were starving. Nadan had answers even though he hadn't been to a nightclub in a couple of years. Gambling took all his time and effort and since his sister died it didn't seem important anymore. He liked the young couple's enthusiasm. He wasn't jealous of them, well, maybe a little bit. And he thought about Alice. Could he go out to dinner with her; go to nightclubs and get home at 7AM and have wild thrilling sex and sleep all day. They might decide to stop partying, to save money together. She would get a job and move in. She had already but she was going away and he felt lonely for a minute or two, and then people came to the desk asking him questions and he brightened up and smiled and joked, his trifecta in the last at Randwick on his mind.

His boss came and gave him a break at 7PM. He rang the automated race results line and found out the bad news on the last in Randwick. He wanted to ask Alice to stay, to help him quit. Only the harness race left now. He rang his home number and she picked up.

'What're doing?' he asked.

'Watching one of your movies.'

'Which one?' he asked.

'*Casino.*'

'Ah, DeNiro.'

'You gamble today?'

'How'd you know?'

'Obvious. I'm still leaving tomorrow.'

'I know.'

'How's work?'

'I like it. I slack off sometimes but I like it. I like telling people not to waste their money on a tour of the harbour but to just catch the ferry to Manly and walk along the beach and where to eat in Potts Point and to go to Glebe and Leichhardt and to walk from Bondi to Coogee or at last to Tamarama along the cliffs.'

'So, you're not a total slacker.'

'I'll see you after midnight. Don't weaken.'

'That's nice you said that.' And she hung up.

She watched the end of the movie and hoped he'd come straight home and that they'd have sex and talk and laugh. She was thinking about scoring. One last time before she left. Catch the train into the city and give someone a call. She could probably score at a pub around here. Kings Cross of course, but she had no money and she thought of what she'd done in the past to get a hit. She'd made it this far. Don't weaken, he said.

Nadan's numbers on the harness trifecta were 1-3-7 boxed. He hadn't looked at the odds of the horses. Nothing like that. Pure guesswork. He rang the results line and the automated voice said, *placings 1-3-7*. And he pumped his fist. Probably get a few hundred, he thought. The voice went through the totes. First place was $26.40. That was big and the placing were high too. Shit! He thought. This could be...and the voice said, *Trifecta on 1-3-7...$8540.25...* Nadan pumped his fist. He was small time. He knew it. But this was a small fortune. Starting over money. Enough to say 'I quit.'

He rang Alice again and she answered and he said, 'I want to come with you.'

'Why? I mean, what happened?'

'I won big.'

'How big?'

'Eight thousand.'

'Best think about it, Nadan. You don't really know me. What I've done. Could do again.'

'We could help each other. I'll buy a cheap car for a few grand and we can get the caravan. Not have to rush about finding jobs.'

'I'll see you when you get back.' And she hung up again.

Nadan's head was spinning. Full of plans for the future. He liked her and he knew she liked him. She said so. He didn't give a stuff about her past. They were both starting over. Fresh starts together on the south coast.

When Chen arrived at ten minutes to midnight, Nadan said a quick goodbye and caught a taxi straight back to Bondi. He noticed there were no lights on in the flat and put the key in the door and opened it to pitch blackness and deadly quiet. He was immediately dispirited, but the bedside lamp came on and Alice was sitting up in bed, topless, with the big Mexican hat on her head and she smiled and held her arms out wide and said loudly, 'Hola!'

Nadan practically runs and dives on the bed, laughing loudly. He stops and looks at her and says, 'You have beautiful breasts. They're gravity-defying, not big but not small and round and...'

'Shut-up, Croatian man.'

'How'd you know?'

'I Googled it.'

'How'd you get into my laptop?'

'I went to the library. I'm surprised you didn't pawn your laptop.'

'I was going to if that trifecta didn't come in. I'll buy a car tomorrow.'

'So, you mean it. You want to come with me.'

'Yes.'

In the morning Nadan makes coffee and they drink it in bed, smoking and making plans and he says to Alice,

'You hardly have any clothes.'

'I thought you might come with me to the house in Erskineville and...'

'No, no way. Leave it behind.' She screws up her face tight and says,

'Just like you're going to leave gambling behind and I checked your closet and you have heaps of t-shirts I could wear. It's still summer for another couple of months and maybe you could buy me a bikini with your winnings and I can buy some stuff. I call the money I get the dole but it's actually sickness benefit. My doctor gave me two months. I'm going to call him up and ask for another two-month certificate, ask him to post it to me.'

'Can he do that?'

'Yeah, I think so.'

'So, what it means is you don't have to prove you looked for work to get your payments.'

'Yeah, getting off heroin is big enough for a while, isn't it.'

After Nadan picked up his cash at the TAB in Bondi Junction, he bought Alice a pre-paid mobile phone and some credit for it. Then they both took the train to the city. Alice had decided to see her doctor before they left, and Nadan had checked out cars online at home before he found what he thought he wanted in a car yard on Parramatta Road. It was on the right-hand side as you head towards Parramatta, about half-a-K past Norton Street. He caught the bus there.

The car he had seen online was an old Ford Falcon sedan, and when he got there he saw the car had Venetian blinds on the back window and he was pretty much sold after that. It had a nice stereo that was out of date but would be loud, and it came with a CD *and* cassette player. He had all his sister's old cassettes but found it hard to listen to them. Maybe it would be different with Alice by his side. He took a short drive with the second-hand dealer sitting in the passenger seat beside him and they agreed on $3000 including all on-road costs, and Nadan was smiling as he drove back into the city to pick up Alice. He stopped and made a call to his boss at the motel telling him that he needed three days off, maybe four. Told his boss he couldn't say why. They weren't friends but Nadan had never let him down. Nadan never had a sick day in two years because he always needed the money and he was a casual even though he worked six days a week, so if he didn't work he didn't get paid.

His boss told him, 'Any more than four days don't come back.' They would be on the road to the south coast by 3PM. Nadan had told Alice he was quitting his job but he wasn't sure, not yet.

Alice was able to go to the doctor's office and get her two-month sickness certificate after her methadone, happy and relieved that it meant no hassles getting Centrelink payments for the next couple of months. She crossed George Street to the Town Hall steps where she was to wait for Nadan. She sat and smoked a cigarette and mucked about with her phone. She didn't have anyone to call. She wanted to call her mum but things became so difficult between the two of them when she was using and now she doesn't trust Alice. Told her, she had to prove herself. Come back when she got her life in order. Tough love her doctor had said it was. She had to re-earn her mother's trust.

'Hi, Alice.'

She looked up and saw Neville and Dominic. She looked back down again and mumbled, 'Hi.'

'Not happy to see us,' Neville said, 'too good for us all of a sudden.' And Dominic smiled his shit-eating grin but she could see he was hurting a bit and then it came from Neville, 'We're heading over to Marrickville. Want to come?'

She sort of did, thought about that feeling of weightlessness after the hit, then the dream-like state and no pain. She hadn't told Nadan everything, some of the things she did, but she said, 'Get lost! Both of you, get lost.'

Neville grabbed her wrist and Nadan saw it as he walked towards Alice. He ran and slapped Neville's hand away and picked Alice up by her forearm and said to Neville and Dominic, 'Piss off, go on, fuck off.'

'Watch it mate,' Dominic said turning nasty.

Nadan knew then what he was facing and he said, 'Fuck off, you junkie piece of shit, and you too,' he said, pointing at Neville. 'Go on, fuck right off or I'll deck you both here on the street.' And he pulled Alice along and they walked off towards where the car was parked on York Street, behind the QVB.

When they got into the car Alice leaned over and hugged him and said, 'Thanks, you were brilliant.'

'Fucking junkie scum,' he said.

'You say that word junkie with so much *vitriol*.'

'Vitriol! A junkie killed my sister. I told you that. And those guys back there, they want to drag you back down. Fuck them.'

'I like the car,' she says and smiles.

'Me too, but don't get me started on that shit. Now, let's go home and pack the car and get the fuck out of Sydney.'

'Have you told the real estate agent you're leaving?'

'I'm going to send him an email asking him to take the rent owed out of my bond and we'll clean the place up before we leave. It's so small it'll only take an hour.'

A few hours later they're in Wollongong, sitting at a café on Burelli Street called Santana Coffee. They're sitting at a table outside holding hands and smoking a cigarette each. The waitress delivers their coffee and Nadan says, 'I want to stay in Kiama tonight. We'll get a motel or a van. I want to see the blowhole.'

'Cool, me too.'

'It's only forty Ks from here. How was that descent into Wollongong, amazing?'

'Yeah, but your new car handled it and it seems like it's travelling well.'

'Yeah, it hasn't missed a beat. You sound so much better, such a different person to who walked into my work.'

'I was desperate, no place to stay and I'm still, oh, forget it. Your boss is going to kill you for taking off.'

'Yeah, he is,' Nadan says, feeling guilty he didn't quit.

They found a motel in Kiama for $95 a night. The motel was on Bong Bong Street, which gave Nadan a laugh, a laugh that went on and on for Alice who said, 'Get over it, it's not that funny.'

The motel was 3 KMs from the blowhole. They were in a downstairs room, the car parked right outside the door. Nadan jumped onto the bed next to Alice and started pulling up her t-shirt but she turned away and said, 'Not now, huh. I'm trying to...I'm stressing about where I'm going to get my methadone. Maybe we should have stayed in Wollongong, it's bigger, and there are more doctors and...'

'Your problem,' Nadan said, 'it's pretty widespread. I reckon for sure there'll be junkies and ex-junkies wherever you go.'

'Wherever *we* go, don't you mean, and I'm *not* a fucking junkie. Ok! Don't talk about me like that. Junkies! Fucking junkies! Shut up, you idiot.'

'Whoa! OK. OK. Let's go for a walk or drive down to the blowhole.'

'You go. I just want to rest.'

Nadan shrugs and says, 'Alright. I'll see you when I get back.' And he walks out the door and starts the car. As he drives out a beat-up dark blue muscle car drives in.

Alice sighs as the door closes. If he calls anyone a fucking junkie again, she thinks, she's going to kill him. She looks in the bar fridge. Empty. She goes to the bathroom and fills a small glass with water and drinks quickly and fills it again and again and drinks the water down. She knows she'll be able to get methadone in Nowra but it is a small place. Will getting the methadone put a stain on her *and* on Nadan?

Alice opens the door and sees the beat-up dark blue car. The boot is open and three doors down a guy with dark, black curly hair, wearing black track pants and a black long-sleeved t-shirt, with bare feet, walks to the boot of the car and he sees Alice but says nothing. She watches him. It's thirty-five degrees but he's got the long sleeves on. She can see his green eyes even from where she's standing. He stops and looks at her, then walks over and says, 'Hi, where's the action around here?'

Alice smiles despite herself and says, 'Don't know, we just arrived.'

'We?' he asks her.

'My friend and I. He went to see the blowhole.'

'I was thinking more like a drink and some other fun.'

'I could go a beer.' She says and the words are out of her mouth before she realizes it.

'I'll be finished unloading the car in five or ten minutes, just knock on the door, sweetheart.'

'Maybe, but we have plans for later.' And Alice closes the door. She knows it. He's got the look. Nadan was right. There are junkies everywhere. The past is always with you. She lies down and closes her eyes.

There's a loud knocking on the door. How long has she been asleep? She looks at the clock. Only five minutes but it feels like hours. She opens the door. The guy with black curly hair and green eyes. The track pants now blue Levi's but still the long sleeves and he has two beers in his hands.

'Nice and cold,' he says and holds one can of beer out to her.

'Thanks,' she says and takes it in her right hand then cracks with her left and says, 'What's your name?'

'Charlie.'

'Nice name, why the long sleeves? It's pretty hot.' She looks at his green eyes, the black pupils still a little constricted and she knows.

Charlie says, 'I got my gear and works in my room.'

'Straight shooter, huh.'

'I knew as a soon as I saw you,' Charlie said.

When Nadan gets back two hours later he has a big pizza and a bottle of coke for them but Alice is gone. Her big bag, the one she had that first night in the motel in Potts Point, it's gone too. He sits down at the little round wooden table and sighs heavily and opens the pizza box.

Charlie and Alice had a blast each, only small doses. Charlie is just starting down this road and it had that six weeks off for Alice. She had a little spew but drifted into the dream zone and she sat on a chair with a green plastic cushion and kept slipping down it when she got the nods. Charlie lay down on the bed and told her Brett Whitely had died of an overdose somewhere around here and she smiled and they drifted in and out of sleep.

Later that night Alice asked if she could lie down beside him, and Charlie smiled, his green eyes shone. She curled around his back as he told her the story of how he got started on the gear. Alice let her hand fall down onto his fly and then undid the top button of his jeans and said, 'I like you, Charlie.'

FREMANTLE

Chris isn't sure exactly what it is about Fremantle that made him move there from Melbourne after having only been there for a week's holiday in summer. You fall in love with a place sometimes. Is it the same as falling in love with a girl? Just that something you can't explain. Like him and Anita.

Chris is on the front beach at Fremantle, near the sandstone fort, sitting by himself, smoking a joint. It's winter and the wind is bitterly cold but he's rugged up. Anita will be here tomorrow. Chris is the advance party. Finding a flat, and he's picked up some work at a café on South Terrace as a barista. He thinks barista is a bit much. He churns out coffee from a machine. It's not rocket science but people seem impressed when he tells them.

Chris joined a theatre group almost straight away. Something he never would have done in Melbourne. Anita: he's not sure what she's going to think. In his mind when he planned this whole thing, Anita wasn't there. He didn't see them walking along South Terrace or at the markets together. He

47

hadn't imagined telling her he wanted to write plays and films and so much more. She saw him as the 'reporter guy' on the local paper, nothing more. He was solid. A good guy. All her friends liked him. He had a passion though. He began to explain a film to Anita one time, what it was about and how much it meant to him and she started laughing, said, *calm down it's only a film.*

He'd met other people here who were, if anything, even more enthusiastic than he was. They were happy to talk about Clint Eastwood's *Play Misty for Me* and how it showed that he was destined to be one of the all-time great filmmakers. This guy, Andrew keeps talking to him about David Lynch, particularly, this one episode of *Twin Peaks* that seems to mesmerise him. Chris laughed but in a good way. He knew the feeling, he just hadn't seen that particular episode.

Anita went to the multiplex. That's an American term because she only wants to see the latest American blockbuster. Australian films were crap, not *The Castle* or *Muriel's Wedding*, but everything else was crap. She shopped at Myer and David Jones and did the grocery shopping at Woolworths or Coles. She wore fashionable shiny suits to her job as a real estate receptionist. She wore short skirts and tights in winter. Melbourne was the centre of the universe. The world's most liveable city. She wanted to get married and have kids right now but she was prepared to go and live in Fremantle for a year because she loved him. Chris didn't know how to cut her loose.

Chris is twenty-five and Anita is twenty-four. They've been living together for two years. He planned his week-long holiday to Fremantle well in advance not knowing the impact it would have on him. He planned it at a time that he knew Anita wouldn't want to leave Melbourne. The 27th of December. Her whole family: parents, brothers and sisters and in-laws. They all went to Sorrento, stayed all close together. Chris hated it and Anita loved it. She gave him permission to go to Fremantle. *I trust you,* she said. Walking around a place he'd never been to before on his own. It was better than the trips with Anita to Thailand, Bali and Europe. He found out about the theatre group on the holiday and they were performing, *Death of a Salesman* when he was there. He nearly flipped out when he went to see it. It was so brilliant.

He walks to Fremantle Station, catches the train to Mosman Park, four stops from Fremantle. It's a short ten-minute walk to this flat in Bond St. He sees it as his flat. One bedroom and a lounge room, up high, with a view to the ocean but not modern or special in any way. He tells himself he's going to call Anita tonight, tell her it's over. Stop it right now before she gets on the plane. He thinks he might have been in love with her for eighteen months, but that thing about explaining the film, it made him think that she had no idea who he really was. Chris cooks himself dinner. An Indian curry. He picked up the ingredients at the Fremantle Markets, wandering through from stall to stall.

7.30PM. If he was going to call he'd have to do it now. In a way, he is looking forward to seeing her. Misses her touch and smile but he just doesn't want her to stay. She's getting in at midday and he doesn't have to work tomorrow. She'll catch a taxi and be here in Mosman Park by 1PM. It'll be too late then, she'll have arrived.

Anita checks the time on the clock on the oven door. 7.30PM. She's nervous. Last time Chris rang she barely got a word in. It's like he's fallen in love with the place but she's getting the plane tomorrow.

Michael, her boss, said, 'Any second thoughts, you can have your old job back. I'll keep it open for another week or two.'

She'd only packed one suitcase. Hadn't told the owner she, or they, weren't moving out. She was going to see Chris but she wasn't going to stay, but maybe she would. She could get another job, she knew she could. Michael, her boss, would give her a great reference. Chris telling her about his job. He was a reporter, not a waiter. They couldn't buy a place if he was only working three days a week as a waiter. She took the lasagne out of the oven. Made a small salad and ate alone at the kitchen table. Chris said he'd made some friends. He'd only been there a month and he wasn't outgoing. Hospitality people no doubt, they were always out drinking and getting stoned. Chris had been like that when they first met but he'd changed. No more party drugs or smoking dope.

She was eating and the phone rang.

'Chris, hi. I'll be there tomorrow, babe. I miss you. Are you alright? Bond St, isn't it? Don't do anything stupid like pop out for cigarettes. You should give up, anyway.'

'No, no. I'll be waiting. I miss you, um, it'll be cool. You'll see. You'll love it.'

'OK, I'm really tired and, um, I miss you. I'm going to hang up. I'm in bed.'

'Good night,' Chris says, turns off his cell phone and lies back on his sofa and lights a cigarette. She won't let him smoke in the flat. She hates drugs. He knows she won't like the new friends he's made. She'll be here tomorrow at 1PM. He has to make a choice right now, it's not too late to call her back, tell her don't come. He turns his cell phone back on.

NORSEMAN

I'm on a Qantas flight from Darwin to Perth, sitting comfortably in the aisle seat. The middle seat is vacant and there is a copy of Bill Bryson's latest travel book about Australia sitting there. The owner is an English girl about twenty-eight or thirty, a lawyer she tells me. She's on holiday and meeting her brother who is backpacking around Australia. She wants to know what I'm doing in Perth.

'I have no idea,' I tell her. 'I'm going to hole up in a motel for a day or two then catch up with a friend, Tim. I know him from Sydney but he lives in Perth now.'

'Oh, you free spirit,' she exclaims, which is not what I expected and I'm not sure if it's sarcasm or not. We chat for a little while longer. She has come from New York but lives in London. I tell her I just spent four months on Elcho Island (Galiwinku), an Aboriginal Community about six hundred kilometres east of Darwin in the Arafura Sea. She doesn't seem very impressed.

I borrow the Bill book to read during the rest of the flight and that's the end of the conversation until she says as we're getting off, 'You should go to Kings Park. They're having this big flower show on the weekend.' And I never see her again.

Waiting for my bags to come out of the carousel drives me crazy. I pick my two small backpacks off the conveyor belt and coins go everywhere, the small zips have come open. Oh! Screw it. Too embarrassing to be crawling around on the floor of the terminal, besides I'm cashed up, for me anyway. Working on Elcho, nothing to spend money on, no gambling, no drinking and no drugs—just cigarettes. I've no idea where to stay so I go over to this noticeboard on the wall of the terminal. It has all these accommodation listings. I choose a motel in East Perth for sixty dollars a night and jump in a cab. It's a Maori guy at the wheel and he's OK. We crap on about the All Blacks and he curses the TV stations because all they show is the AFL.

'I understand your pain, brother,' I say. 'I'm a rugby league fiend and I hear they show the matches at midnight or later unless you have Foxtel.'

He drops me at the motel and says, 'Kia ora, brother.'

I'm going to take a couple of days to look around Perth, have a few bets and take in the sights, get on the train to Fremantle and then it will be Tim time. He's a big bloke and a big drinker. The last text I had from him, he said he was living with a local girl, Tracy. Maybe she has a friend?

In the morning I'm pointed in the direction of Murray St by the beautiful young receptionist on duty. I head off on foot. Whenever I go to a new place I always like to walk everywhere. I just think it helps you get a better handle on the size and layout of the city or town. I make it to Murray St via a nice park and Wellington St but I keep looking for a recognisable CBD. I mean like Melbourne or Sydney but there isn't any. Hay St isn't much different to Murray St but St Georges Terrace shows me a bigger, brighter, more business-like Perth.

I wander back to Murray St and find a not too busy café

opposite the Commonwealth Bank, in the mall. I call Tim but get voice mail. I let him know where I'm staying. My coffee arrives and the waiter looks like he must have had a tough night or a bad morning. Next, I go to an internet café, email some friends and check on the employment site, Seek. I notice a job for a 'retail assistant' in a place called Norseman. What takes my interest is that Norseman is described as remote. I have a plan to go and live and work in Asia, probably Bangkok or Saigon, but I know I'll need big savings. This could be like Elcho, nothing to spend my money on but also a unique take on WA. I call the number and I get a receptionist who patches me through to this English guy and an interview is arranged for this afternoon at 12PM at an office in Hay St. It's a Monday in September, 2003, and starting to get pretty hot. The air is dry, almost arid. The football finals are on. Tim calls me as I'm walking back to the motel.

'Maaate, how are you?' he asks loudly. 'Welcome to WA, the state of drinking.' I fill him in on where I'm staying and he says, 'I have an RDO. I'll pick you up.'

'I have an interview at Midday. How about 2PM.'

'Alright, listen, mate, check out of the motel. Come and stay in Cottesloe, at my place. Hey, guess what. Stuart is over here. He's working in a hotel in Freo.'

'That's great. I'll see you at two. Let me think about the other thing. Gotta go. See ya.' I don't want to be tied into anything. If I stay at his place I have to obey the rules of friend-ship. I can't just take off when I like. If I'm over something or had enough to drink, I can't just take off for *home*. And I really like Stuart, he's a good bloke, so I'll be glad to see him. All three of us knocked around Bondi together.

The interview is more like booking a ticket in a travel agency than applying for a job. The Englishman tells me about Norseman. It was a boom mining town that pretty much went bust although I did a Google search on it myself and the mine still operates.

'You can buy a house there now for $10,000. We'll refund all travelling costs if you stay more than three months. You catch a train from East Perth to Kalgoorlie and then take a bus to Norseman. The train I believe is seven to eight hours and another three or four on the bus.'

'You're telling me I have the job.'

'If you want it, yes. I can see you've moved around a lot from your CV and you have to do a bit of everything out there. They have a motel but the main employment is in the road-house. Road trains and travellers coming through twenty-four hours a day.' I ask for twenty-four hours to think about it and he agrees. Sounds like they're desperate for workers but that doesn't put me off. It's in the middle of bloody nowhere anyway. I have a change of clothes in my backpack and I call Tim and let him know I'm taking the train to Fremantle, and he agrees and tells me he'll contact Stuart and we agree to meet at the Bar Orient on High St.

The train out to Fremantle is a pretty good service. Around Cottesloe, some three or four stops from Fremantle you start getting glimpses of the ocean and then the white sandy beaches. I like it a lot and wonder about Norseman. An old gold mining town gone to seed. Or is it? I stroll around Fremantle and it reminds me of Bondi in size and the village feel it has to it. It's a modern place with almost the feel of a country town. I eat at McDonald's near the beach on an outside table. At a few minutes to 2PM I walk around past the old fort on the beach and across the railway tracks to High St and into the Bar Orient.

Much handshaking and backslapping takes place and we laugh and talk of Bondi. Good times. Tim says, 'Mate, I love it over here, the beaches, the weather and the rent is cheaper. Me and Tracy are talking about buying a place. I have money left over at the end of the week, something I never had in Sydney.' I think that might have more to do with the unseen Tracy but I don't say it.

Then Stuart starts up the WA band and says, 'Nick, I've been here about six months, started out just doing some casual painting when they were renovating and they offered me the night manager's job. I love it over here.'

'Get off those night shifts, Stuart,' I say, 'they'll kill you. Trust me I know.' Then I tell them, 'I've been offered a job in Norseman. Know anything about it?'

Blank stares and Stuart says, 'If I know you, I bet it's in the middle of nowhere.'

'If you call 950km South/east of Perth nowhere then you're spot on.'

Tim has a go, 'Jesus, mate. You're surrounded by paradise and you're going out there. The gold rush is over, mate. Even Alan Bond knows that.'

Much laughter and a few more beers and I tell them I'm shipping out tomorrow and thank Tim for the offer of somewhere to stay but I'm closer to East Perth Station than he is and I walk to Fremantle railway station while calling the English bloke on my cell phone and telling him I'll be on the train and bus tomorrow and he says to me, 'Oh, the bus is only just over two hours. I'm told they show a movie.' I buy my ticket to Norseman at Fremantle railway station and the man tells me they're updating 'The Prospector' (the train) in June 2004 and it will be much better with movies and music like plane flights, which doesn't do me any good. I have an early night back at the motel. I'll be seeing those Bondi boys again when I pass back through on my way to south-east Asia.

In the morning on the station, I almost don't go but I think of Bangkok and Saigon and parts unknown and what a great adventure it will be. I also think about Norseman, population hovering around 1000. I think of it back when the mine was booming and wonder how many people lived there back then. I've never worked in a roadhouse before either, and I step on the train and find a comfortable window seat. I try and sleep but can't, so I listen to this old walkman I have and try and find interesting radio stations (an old habit of mine) but the reception isn't too good. I press the call button above me just to find out what happens and this lovely girl in a nice uniform asks me what I'd like and I stare at her blankly and she hands me a menu. It ain't Qantas first class but I order a sausage roll and a can of coke and the train stops after about three hours to pick up some passengers and for a break and me and the other smokers sprint for the door and suck down as many of those babies as is possible in fifteen minutes and then it's back on for the long haul into Kal. When we arrive, it's nearly dark and I call ahead to the roadhouse and speak to the manager. He knows who I am, which settles me down a bit, and says he'll meet the bus. Cool. I wait fifteen minutes and the bus to Norseman pulls in and it is dark now.

The movie is *Rio Bravo* starring John Wayne, Dean Martin, Ricky Nelson and the beautiful Angie Dickinson. I love this film and the lights are off and there are only three other passengers. It's a brilliant finish to my long and sometimes painful journey. The pain being the boredom. I step off the bus in Norseman, population now 800 (that's what the sign said), and take a good look around.

Service station with many, many pumps. I see a sign that says 'trucks only' for a number of the pumps and no-one comes up to me and shakes my hand. I sit on a log fence for a few minutes. Nothing. I was the only one who got off. The bus continued to Esperance. I walk into the service station. They have a hot buffet going with a bain-marie. I'm pretty hungry.

There are lots and lots of aisles filled with Twisties and chips and chocolates; souvenir tea towels and beef jerky and a public internet coin-operated machine. I take a seat in the little diner eating area waiting for someone to appear so I can order some food. No-one does. I walk up to the cash register at the front and there's an office close by. I knock on the door. This big barrel-chested man in yakka pants and an orange fluoro vest (the kind road workers wear) says, 'What's up, mate? Can I help you?'

'I'm Nick Garides.'

'And that means something because?'

'I have a job here. I'm looking for Mike Rogers.'

He stares at me for a few seconds and then says, 'Right, sorry, so many people come and go from this joint. I spoke to you on the phone.'

'Yeah. Two hours ago,' I say and he tells me that I start tomorrow on the cash register at the front where people pay for fuel and the souvenirs.

'7AM. My daughter, Missy, will be training you. We're gonna put you up in the motel for a couple of nights until someone moves out of one of the staff houses.' He gives me a key and tells me I can eat what I want from the buffet. Just tell them I work here now. I introduce myself at the buffet and eat up big on sweet and sour chicken and rice. Afterwards, I walk off in the direction of the motel and find my room and, yeah, like any other highway motel room. I shower and crash into sleep.

In the morning I walk across to the roadhouse, and even at this early part of the day, I'm getting attacked by flies. Sticky black flies that remind me of Yulara in the NT where I worked for a short period of time, except these flies are bigger and more obnoxious. The girl at the cash register is beautiful and around twenty-five, I reckon. I introduce myself and we shake hands and she says, 'I'm Missy,' and she starts going through everything and there are about a million keys on the cash register and she says, 'I can't really show you until we get some customers. Don't worry, it'll get busy. We get to choose what CDs we can play, just not too loud. Have a look and choose something.'

I go for Powderfinger, Odyssey Number Five. After a while I start to sing along, it's a bad habit of mine and I have a very bad singing voice, and Missy says, 'You have a great voice,' while smiling broadly.

I take it and say, 'What do you for entertainment around here?'

'There are dances at the RSL and the pub and other stuff.' The roadhouse does get busy and Missy gets on well with all the truckies and I'm just trying to do my work and not screw up and the day goes quickly.

She starts walking back to the motel with me and I ask, 'Where do you live?'

'With dad in a house on Roberts St.'

'Have you always lived here?'

'Yes.'

'Never wanted to go to Perth or Kalgoorlie?'

'I'm not...I've been of course, but I've always lived here.'

'I don't get it. Why are you here?'

'You're here.'

'That's a frustrating answer.'

'Want to make me a drink or coffee in your room?'

'Can we take a walk down the main drag first? Is that what Norseman locals say, the main drag.'

'No, we say we don't give the time of day to facetious bastards.'

'I'm sorry. I have this very dry not very nice sense of humour.'

'Apology accepted. Come on, follow me.'

We cross the motel car park and go right back almost to the roadhouse and then turn onto Roberts St (the main drag). There is no nature strip, the side of the road is dirt, and trees line the road. The flies don't seem too bad now. It's a big wide street and rather attractive in a kind of deserted country town way.

'That's my house,' she says, pointing to a respectable-looking, white weatherboard home. There are brick homes too, well built and sturdy, but there's still this deserted atmosphere. I mention it to Missy and she says, 'People live in these houses and they are nice houses. I don't get what you're saying.'

'The guy who interviewed me for the job said that you could buy a house here for $10,000. Is that true?'

'Oh yeah, you probably could but not my house. I mean dad's house.' We pass McIvor St on the right and a big house with a long driveway and steel garage and further on where there are no empty blocks and the public swimming pool is on the left but it's not open and Missy's starting to look pissed off. There's a statue of a horse or donkey on the left before the round-a-bout and she says, 'Let's go back. You can see the town centre and the pub tomorrow or later on.'

'What's up? Are you alright?'

'I don't know how to put this. Um, I get a lot of shit from the locals for always hanging out with the staff, but we get all kinds of people through here and I know all the locals back to front. Right now we have an English couple and this guy from New Zealand and others from all over have been here.'

'Is the grief from the guys or girls?'

'Both. C'mon, let's go back. Do you have music?'

'Just a small CD player.'

Back at my room she says, 'Don't move out of the room.

Just tell dad you like it. We never get full and you won't have to share.'

'Have you ever thought of moving to Perth?' I ask her.

'Not that again,' she says. 'Oh, you have Pete Murray, Sheryl Crowe *and* Luka Bloom.'

'You know yesterday I was in Fremantle and Pete Murray was playing at a pub there tonight. Wouldn't you like to be there?'

'Oh shut up! Shut up about how great it is everywhere but here! I like you, Nick, but just shut up about that stuff. I'm not stupid. I probably know more about music and books and films than you ever dreamed of. This is a new age. I have the internet. I get whatever is current the minute, the second I want it. I can download anything. New music or films and book reviews and house prices in Perth. You're thirty years old and you don't have two cents to your name but I don't keep reminding you of it.'

'How do you know what...'

'Oh, come on. Would you be here if you didn't?'

'I came here to save money. I have close to $4000 and I want another $4000 because I want to go and live in Bangkok or Saigon. I came here because I have a goal I want to get to.'

'Oh wow! $4000. Big deal. Why don't you buy a house here? That's what you meant, isn't it. This place is so crap you can buy a house for $10,000.'

'I don't want to argue with you. Pete Murray or Luka Bloom?'

And she sings, '*My name is Luka; I live on the second floor.*'

'Oh, very cute,' I say, but I have the biggest smile on my face.

The next morning I wake at 6AM and the room is stuffy, so I pull on a pair of jeans and open the door which has a terrific view of the car park and the other motel units. Missy and I played music for a couple of hours and she talked a lot about life in Norseman and how this guy, Lincoln, broke her heart. He was from Adelaide and had hitched-hiked across the Nullarbor Plain and walked into the roadhouse looking for work. Promised her the earth and then left at midnight one night with a waitress from the motel.

I mostly listened, and when I opened the door for her to leave, she kissed me softly on the lips and said, 'See you, tomorrow, Nick. Thanks for listening.'

She left at nine so I got to bed early and promised myself one of my mantras was going to be *Early to bed, early to rise. Save money.* I shower and make instant coffee, smoke a few cigarettes. Go to the diner for breakfast and have three bowls of Rice Bubbles and about six pieces of toast and more coffee and a final cigarette as Missy walks towards me.

'All ready for training?' she asks, and I mumble a yes.

We take over the cash register from Neal, an English guy who has been here for four weeks.

'I'm leaving in two weeks,' he says. And I quickly count the till so he can go.

It gets busy straight away. I can't believe it and I get some grief from a truckie when I stuff up his bill from the diner and he says, 'Get with it, mate. I need you to be fast. Time is money in this game. C'mon.'

He makes me nervous and Missy steps in and fixes it up and gives him some cheek and he loves it and says, 'Sorry, mate, but I need you to be fast.' And I feel like saying, 'stop talking to me and you'd be a lot faster.'

Ten minutes later I answer the phone and this voice says, 'Ronny here, order me two serves of chips, burn the bastards, and I'll be there in five.'

I tell Missy and she says, 'Simmo. Mad bastard. Those stories of truck drivers on speed. That's Ronny Simpson.'

Everything is going pretty well. I have the cash register with its millions of buttons and keys pretty much down and there's a *Best Songs of 2002* CD in the drive, and I'm humming, not singing, and this guy with long hair and loose baggy harem pants walks in. His girlfriend is in a tie-dye T-shirt and cargo shorts and I give them a big smile and say, 'How're doing? Where have you come from?'

And this guy looks at his girlfriend and rolls his eyes and says, 'Where have you come from? The most asked question at the Norseman Roadhouse,' and he says it with heavy sarcasm and I'm about to give him blast when Missy just pats my bum and smiles at me and I let it go.

He pays for his petrol and buys cigarettes and I ask him, 'Where are you headed?' And he starts the roll of the eyes again but sees me smiling and walks out.

'Kill em with kindness,' Missy says. I wanted to say to him, 'You don't know me; you don't know anything about me. Not why I'm here or where I'm from.' His sarcasm hit a nerve and I put it together with what Missy said about me being thirty and only having two cents to my name and I want to head overseas and then what. I think about it for the whole shift. I can't shake it.

'Feel like a beer?' Missy asks at the end of the shift.

'At the pub?'

'No, your room. Tomorrow night we'll go to the pub. You have the Saturday off to sleep in.'

'You're planning my life are you?'

'I don't want the local girls seeing you.'

'Oh right,' I say and I can't quite tell if she's stirring me or not.

'I have a six-pack at home. I'll bring it over,' she says.

I meet Gloria as she arrives to take over the shift; she's from

Stirling, a suburb in Perth and she says, 'I'm leaving in two weeks.' And, 'Are you in the staff house or the motel?'

'Motel.'

'Oh, don't worry. It's not so bad here, just don't stay too long.'

'How long have you been here?'

'Two months.'

'Oh, OK, taking your own advice. I have to go, so, see ya.'

On the way back to my room I stop in at the motel reception to ask about using the phone in my room and how much the calls cost. I introduce to myself to Warren at the front desk and Monica, the motel manager, comes out and shakes my hand and we all have a little chat and Monica goes back into the office and Warren says, 'I'm leaving in two weeks.'

'Oh, um, great,' I say and walk out and see Missy walking ahead of me to the room. I should have said that Missy is short and compact with shiny black hair that she wears (so far) in a thick ponytail. I watch her bum sway from side to side as she walks and smile. Her eyes are black too and she has thick eyelashes and eyebrows. I see her knocking on my door and still can't shake that bad feeling I got from that smartarse in the roadhouse.

I rest my hand on her waist as we walk inside. She turns and holds up the six-pack.

'Oh, Swan Lager,' I say.

'You should be thankful. This is my treat.'

'You always speak your mind don't you?'

She pulls two cans off the plastic ring one at a time and places them on the small, round, wooden table and we sit like we're about to have dinner together on the two metal chairs with their orange plastic cushions under our arses.

'To Norseman!' I say.

'Cheers,' she says softly, thinking I'm being sarcastic, and then asks me to put on some music. I put on Lloyd Cole and the Commotions and she says as he sings, *Love is all you need.*

'Who is this?'

'Lloyd Cole, like it?'

'Yeah, what's the name of the album?'

'*Rattlesnakes.*'

'Cool.'

We drink and talk and laugh for a couple of hours and she says, 'I better get back. Dad's going to Perth tomorrow and I promised I'd have dinner with him.' I nod. I don't want her to leave. I think she knows it and says, 'Do you like me?'

'You mean do I like you in that way?'

She doesn't answer the question, she says, 'You know a lot of the locals make out I'm some kind of tramp because I always hang out with the new male workers who come here, but I was only ever with the one guy and *he* left *me.* I liked you the minute you walked into the roadhouse. That's never happened to me before.' I don't know what to say and she says, 'It's OK. I'll see you tomorrow.' And she throws an empty can into the small waste basket on the other side of the room.

'Good shot,' I say but it sounds really hollow. She closes the motel room door softly behind her when she leaves.

I bring *Rattlesnakes* to work the next morning and I say to Neal, the English guy, 'Only thirteen days left, Neal.' He shrugs and walks out. I thought I was being friendly.

Missy walks in and she sees the CD and says straight away, 'You can play that as long as you don't sing along.' I smile and nod. She adds, 'I'm going to let you do everything today, training is over. Dad's gone to Perth already, so believe it or not, I'm running the place. I'll be in the office if you get stuck.' I simply nod again. Three trucks are filling up and three people just walked in and the rest of the day is flat out until 3PM. I had my lunch standing up at the cash register and had to beg Missy to get a smoke break.

I'm walking out and she grabs me by the arm and says, 'Come to the house for dinner. I'm cooking. I have some wine too.' A few of the motel workers and a group of people from the staff house had invited me to the pub. There are about fifteen to twenty people working here. Housemaids, short-order cooks, receptionists and barman, and the maintenance guy, and I've barely spoken to anyone and I say, 'I was asked to the pub.' She looks away from me and I think about it. Who gives a stuff about the pub.

'I'll come over for dinner but we should go to the pub after that.'

'OK. Be at my place at seven.' And I walk out.

I get to her house right on seven and it's still pretty hot. The house is hot too because she's cooking and I say, 'Any air-conditioning?'

'I'll put the ceiling fan on and it's nice to see you too.'

'What're you cooking?'

'This Malaysian chicken curry. I got the curry paste at this supermarket in Kal about two weeks ago. Want a beer?'

'Yeah.'

She goes to the fridge and brings over a VB and I smile and take it and crack the ice-cold can. She sits next to me on the sofa and puts her hand on my thigh and I turn to face her and she kisses me on the mouth and I kiss her back and she says, 'I just wanted to get that out of the way.'

The Malaysian curry is great and she plays a lot of her dad's old soft rock CDs. Stuff like Foreigner, Status Quo and Toto, and I don't mind. I even dance badly with her and we kiss a lot and don't go to the pub and she asks me to stay the night.

The next morning she has to go to work and I have the day off. I sneak back to my motel room, but along the way meet the housemaids and some other staff and they all give me a hard time about not turning up to the pub and staying the night at 'the manager's house.' There are no secrets in Norseman.

Her dad went to Perth for three weeks and I stayed at the house the whole time. I've been here three months now, living in the motel room on my own but with Missy coming over almost every night. One morning I go to work and get there ten minutes early because I'm training a new staff member on the cash register. The wheel has turned the full circle. All those who said they were leaving have left and others have come and gone in that time too.

Sheila, the new staff member is about forty and a big woman. More big-boned than overweight and she asks me, 'How long have you been here?' I tell her and she seems to be waiting for me to tell her how much longer but I don't.

Two weeks later it is 3PM and I'm sitting on the front lawn of the house that Missy and I have rented and Missy opens the front gate and comes and sits next to me and asks, 'How long have you been here?'

'Over three months,' I say.

She asks, 'When are you leaving?'

'Never.'

PARKVILLE

I'm staying at the Parkville Motel, Brunswick, and it's all good. I haven't come across anyone; then, there he is, right in front of me. Standing outside the Barkly Square Shopping Centre on Sydney Road, Brunswick. The man they call The Doctor (as in Doctor Feelgood). He looks at me, a smile starts to spread across his face in recognition. I stop walking for a moment; he grabs me, bear hugs me in front of the whole street.

'Where you been, man? I thought you were dead.'

'Sydney.'

'Hiding in the open like,' he says.

'Yeah, something like that.'

'You reincarnated mother...I thought you were dead.'

'You said that, Doc. What're doing with yourself?'

'For work like?'

'Yeah.'

'Growing hydro, mate. I got a great setup. Can't grow the stuff quick enough and...'

'Jesus, Doc, keep it down, would you?'

'Sorry, mate, you know me.'

The Doctor is wearing blue footy shorts, thongs and a red flannelette shirt topped off with a brutal mullet haircut.

For the past year, I'd been living in Sydney, in Meadowbank. A very quiet and peaceful part of Sydney as the name suggests. A bit of an unknown delight, or maybe that's because I was from Melbourne and didn't know shit. I lived around the corner from a tiny shopping centre that had a milk bar, video store, Italian restaurant, and a Chinese joint. There was a small ferry stop in a secluded park. The ferry took you to Darling Harbour along the Parramatta River. There were never more than three or four people at the ferry stop, although I did make my journeys out of peak hour times. I got a call Jako was in Barwon Prison and I came home.

'Listen, Doc, I'm meeting someone and...'

'No worries mate. And hey, don't worry about Jako, he's inside. I gotta go to Coles, get some food in. Here, take my mobile number down.'

He reads it out. I put it straight into my phone, and for a few seconds, I feel lousy about blowing him off, but he slaps my shoulder, walks through the automatic doors of the shopping centre, and disappears. The Doctor, *growing hyrdo* as he put it.

I keep walking up Sydney Road on the right-hand side, past the chemist warehouse, Hot Potato $2 Shop, looking to my right and left. Bikes everywhere. I reckon there are more bikes per capita in Brunswick than anywhere else in the world.

Sydney Road is bustling with people. I keep walking. I walk past the yellow sign belonging to Two Little Pigs that says 'coffee', but I keep walking and slip into Tom Phat, a Thai restaurant that opens early on the weekends. It always did great coffee too, which is weird for a Thai place, but there is another reason too. I order a strong latte from a girl with a long nose and wide-set brown eyes, slim and tall. I watch her walk to the coffee machine. She's wearing see-through harem pants and a black singlet.

I stare openly at her and she asks me, 'Sugar?'

'No thanks.' She puts the coffee down and I ask her, 'Does Philippa still work here?'

'Yeah, how do you know her?'

'I used to come in here all the time about a year ago.'

'Uh-huh, and you two were friends?'

'Yeah.'

'She's working on Monday. We open at 11 on weekdays.'

'Ok, thanks.'

'Hey, what's your name?'

'Adam.'

On Monday, I walk into Tom Phat at 11.15AM, and there she is, Philippa, just like she'd been one year ago. Long, wavy, red hair and, I hate this word, ethereal, but damn it, that's what she was, goddam ethereal, out of this world. Shining light blue eyes like a cloudless sky. My heart beat a little faster, my palms got sweaty, she turned and saw me and that smile.

The last time I saw Jako was in the tiny flat I lived in on Pearson Street. He was lecturing me on the finer points of dope dealing.

'You need to pay me more heed, young man.'

He talked like that sometimes, like a school teacher from the 1950s, only he never got past year eight in school. Maybe he got it from watching movies.

Anyway, I said, 'Indeed, Jako, indeed,' taking the piss a bit, but he stood up in his cut-off denim shorts and blue singlet, muscles like steel bars on his arms, his huge barrel chest puffed out, the veins in his neck, face and forehead popping out like crazy, sweat pouring off him.

He yelled, 'Fuck your indeed, you scum! Show me some respect, you shit!' He grabbed me and held my face right up next to his stinking cigarette breath mouth, then threw me aside like discarded rubbish onto the floor. It scared the shit outta me but it didn't stop me stealing his dope and money and taking it to Sydney. Hiding in the open, as the Doctor had also said. I knew the Doctor was cool because he hated Jako as much as me.

'Hello, stranger,' Philippa said, all natural and calm like it hadn't been a year since I called and told her some guy called Jako might want to kill me. 'Trish said you came in the other day.'

I shrugged my shoulders. 'We're good. You're not angry.'

'You're not as memorable as you think.'

'Can I have a strong latte?'

'Sure,' and she pointed to the end of a row of tables along the wall opposite and said, 'Go sit way down there. The lights are off until we get busy later. I'll bring your coffee and we can talk for five or ten minutes.'

'Thanks.' I walk past the open kitchen, take a seat. I wait and she brings my coffee. I can smell her peppermint tea.

She sits down all angelic-like, smiles and says, 'You're back for good?'

'I am.'

'Your friend Doc came in, he said to tell you to call him.'

'How did he know, ah, old Doc, he's not stupid. He knew I'd come looking for you.'

'You better call him.'

'I will.'

'What happened to the guy who wanted to kill you?'

'He's in jail.'

'How much did you steal from him?'

'Forty-thousand and change.'

'When you told me a year ago you were leaving, I felt like maybe I didn't know you at all. I know we smoked a little grass together but you're a full-on dealer and you stole from your supplier. Who are you?'

'I didn't think. I mean I didn't think through the consequences when I did it. I was mad at him, furious because he embarrassed me when he tossed me round like a rag doll, but he's in jail now. That's why I came back and to see you.'

I sipped on my coffee, felt like a cigarette.

'I know what you're thinking,' she said. 'We can sit out the front and smoke. I've been given fifteen minutes.' We walk through the café to the seats outside, find the last two seats, she hands me a pack of Alpine. I take one.

'When we were kids at school, say ten or eleven years old, we used to say that if you smoked menthol cigarettes you became sterile only we didn't really know what sterile meant.'

She stares at me.

'I thought it was funny.'

'Yeah, it was hilarious,' she says and starts laughing. I laugh with her and in that instant I fall back in love with her.

'Meet me in my room at the Parkville tonight?'

71

'Motel assignations with a drug dealer. Oh my, I don't know.'

'Oh, come on.'

'I was joking. How about seven tonight?'

'That's great.'

Philippa knocks on my door right on 7PM. I open it and she's wearing this great royal blue mini dress with white trim on the neck and at her wrists, she's got a black umbrella she's shaking the water off and I grab her hand and say, 'You look like a movie star.'

'Which one?'

'Oh no, you're one of a kind, like no-one else.'

'Such a sweet boy for a drug dealing thief.'

I close the door, go and sit on one of the black plastic chairs; she sits on the bed her legs dangling off the end, asks me, 'What did you do with the money and dope you stole?'

'I still have the money but I ran out of dope. I sold a bit here and there and used it myself. I have a couple of joints left only.'

'What kind of people stay here?'

'Drug dealers, bikies, thieves, assassins.'

'Is that a joke like the sterile thing?'

'Honestly, I haven't noticed anyone although the house-maid was very friendly and inquisitive.'

'How nice for you.'

We don't say anything for a while, then she says, 'Let's go away with your money. To Asia. To Thailand. We could live like royalty in Thailand for a year and by that time things might have blown over for you.'

Shit, I think. Normally, I'm the one with the wild ideas.

'Look, people like Jako, they're different. They don't make

sense. If he gets out. When he gets out, he'll still want to kill me.'

'We could keep travelling. Go to Europe. If we came back to Australia we could go and live in WA. I hear Fremantle is great. Or a small town.'

'You'd do that with me?'

'Maybe. If you told me you loved me and asked me to come with you.'

She lay down flat on the bed, her legs still dangling off the end. I walk over and lean down with both hands on either side of her breasts, kiss her on the mouth, gently lay down on top of her.

I'm sitting up in bed smoking a cigarette. Philippa is sitting next to me under the covers, her hip bone just touching me, she's talking about how work gives her the shits sometimes. There's a knock at the door.

'Doc,' I say, 'I told him to drop off some weed.'

I get out of bed, step into my jeans, walk across the floor, open the door. Jako is standing there and he thumps his flat hand into my chest. I stumble back and he comes in and closes the door.

'Get out of bed, put some clothes on,' he says to Philippa. She stares at him and he says firmly, 'Now, get out of bed, now, get dressed and stand in the kitchenette.'

She looks at me and I nod. She slips out of the bed, starts putting her dress on. Jako walks across to me and I put my hands up like a coward, scared stiff, he grabs my left ear and twists it hard like it's a bottle top. The pain is excruciating and it keeps increasing as he twists and squeezes my ear harder and harder. I slump to my knees, my hands still in the air pleading.

'Where's the money, dipshit?' Jako asks coldly, 'the money *and* the dope.'

'I...'

He slaps my face hard twice.

'How'd I know you were here?' Jako asks me.

I don't say anything. I can see Philippa out of the corner of my eye, dressed now, holding her arms around her waist tightly.

'How'd I know you were here?'

'Doc,' I say.

'Not Doc. Who called you in Sydney? Think back.'

'Lino.'

'Yeah, Lino. You wanted to believe I was gone so much, you believed a junkie like Lino and the Doc took the bait too.'

I nod my head; he slaps my face twice again, my head jerks back and forth and I know Philippa is watching me be humiliated. He pulls out a gun, puts it to my head and something flashes to my left, Philippa stabs him with fork! It's sticking out of his neck.

Jako turns and looks at her. 'You finished?' And pulls the fork out of his neck. You can see three dots of blood opening up, starting to trickle down his neck. He says to her, 'Get back over there.' And he slaps me hard in the face again, says, 'Where's the money?'

'In my bag.'

He looks around. Sees the hard purple suitcase on wheels standing in the corner of the motel room, turns to Philippa, says, 'Open it.'

She looks at me and I nod. She walks over to it and fiddles with the lock and there's a knock at the door. Doc opens the door, walks in, says, 'The door was open...Oh.'

Jako smiles at him, says, 'Shut the door. Join the party, Doc.'

Doc closes the door still wearing those footy shorts and he looks at me with the gun at my head, swallows. Jako says to him,

'Stand over there next to her.' Then to Philippa again, 'Open it.' She tries to open it but can't and I remember I have the keys in my pocket.

Philippa says, 'It's locked.'

Jako raises his eyes to the roof for a second. Doc charges him like a rugby player, knocks the gun out of his hand. I jump on Jako, hold him down, but he's bucking like a bronco so I start gouging his fucking eyes. Doc is scrambling round on the floor for the gun. Jako makes one huge effort and bucks me off, but Doc picks up the gun and cracks Jako over the head with it. He drops like a fucken sinker into the ocean. I look at Philippa and she's frozen.

Doc says, 'Grab your stuff. Let's get out of here.'

I walk quickly to Philippa, kiss her on the lips and say, 'You OK? You're OK?'

She nods and I grab her hand and my suitcase and we run to Doc's old Holden.

The Doc took us back to his place and it took us a few days to get over it. Me and Philippa not looking each other in the eye. We checked the news services for the next couple of days but there were no reports of a man being bashed at the Parkville Motel and I'd given the owner a false name when I checked in. There was no way in the world Jako would have reported it. Philippa went to her mum's place for a couple of days. Jako didn't know where the Doc lived, and besides Doc had aligned himself with some pretty heavy dudes and it was these heavy dudes he was growing the hydroponic dope for.

Philippa and I bought tickets to Thailand and on to the UK. We would be officially on the Doc drove us out to the airport. At the gate just before we left he said, 'Keep a low profile, man.'

'Like you, Doc.'

'Yeah, you know me, the soul of discretion.'

PAWN

Geraldton. Western Australia. Australia. Population, 20,000. Stardate... August 20, 2008. The motel with the horseracing tiles in the kitchen. Brown, semi-shagpile carpet from a time long, long ago. A little down on my luck. Bussed it in from Port Hedland, rock hard mining town, where I worked; correction, where I was a wage slave in a very average pub.

I arrived in the early hours of the morning and had made arrangements to pick up the key outside the motel room door, under a rock or something. When I got there, the key was in the door and a note on the kitchen table to 'fix us up' in the morning, meaning cash-type money had to be given. I was waiting on the severance pay from that last job to arrive, due in exactly two hours. My pay normally went into my bank account at 4AM. Yeah, I'm into the habit of accessing the funds as soon as they arrive because I'm usually broke and hanging out for cigarettes. Thank God these towns have service stations or roadhouses because I was starving too.

I had a shit-fight with the bus driver when he pulled into

Port Hedland. I had a bike with me and when I booked the ticket the guy said there was no need to take the front wheel off the bike, which is what you usually have to do, so they can store it away easier. So, of course, when he gets off the bus, he says, 'Take the front wheel off.' I tell him what the guy said and he says to me, 'I'm the bloody bastard that has to stow the shit thing away. Take the bloody wheel off.' And it's a scheduled meal break stop so the whole busload had a laugh at me, and to make matters worse, I don't have a spanner or whatever the hell it is you use, so I have to ask 'Mr Happy' driver for one and he goes through this big shrug of the shoulders and rolls his eyes at a couple of young girls and I'm public enemy number one. Shit. When I got off the bus at 2AM in Geraldton, I was the only one getting off, so I made a big deal of taking my time, but the driver practically buckled the back wheel of the bike getting it out so 2-0 to the bus driver.

Anyway, at 4AM, I walk down from the motel, which is perched on a hill at the entrance to Geraldton and check my account. Only $20 in it. So I withdraw the twenty, cursing the bastards that they haven't put the pay into my account. I buy a packet of Longbeach forties, cigarettes, and a box of Nutrigrain cereal and milk. I should be kept in coffee satchels by the motel, which begs the question, how in the hell do I pay them? I work it out walking up the hill. It's Saturday morning, so the guy who does the pay at the pub where I worked won't be in. I'll have to wait until Monday to abuse him and tell him to get that $800 into my account. I'll find a pawn shop and put the bike in over the weekend. It's nearly brand new, so I should get $100 to keep me going and I'll tell the owner of the motel what happened. Give him my old boss's phone number at the pub to confirm the cash is coming. What a way to live. Bloody-hell.

Midday, I poke my head out from under the blanket. Better get moving. If there is a pawn shop it may only be open for half a day on Saturdays. There's a local phone book and the pawn shop is on the main street into town. Probably passed it on the way in. I go to the reception area and explain to the manager. He's a short stocky guy in brown slacks and a blue cardigan over a body shirt (remember them?).

I'm rather amazed when he takes the whole story with a laugh and says, 'No worries. I don't need the phone number. Just fix it up on Monday. By 3PM now mind.' Country people. God love them. I glide down the hill on my bike, the back way, not down the highway. A big car dealer. Some small industrial area. Fish and chip shop, and as I enter the main drag I spy a Bookie on my left. I turn right on the trundle and check off the numbers on the buildings. I brought along a small CD Walkman-type thing and a dozen CDs just in case. You just can't tell with pawnbrokers. They might gobble up the portable CD player and give me a $100 for that and say they don't want the bike. I've been caught out before. I pass a big pub that advertises a skimpy bar. Weird. I came across them in Port Hedland but didn't indulge. Something weird about being served a beer by a girl in her underwear and topless.

The pawnbroker's is called 'Last Chance Pawnbrokers', and yes, it could be mine. He admires my CDs.

'Bloody good condition.' On the spot I decide to keep the bike. It's a fair hike into town. I show him the portable CD player. 'Very nice,' he says, '$150 the lot, I'll hold them for thirty days.' Sweet.

I trundle back into town and try to find some cheap accommodation. A pub just on the edge of the main town area on the road closest to the beach has rooms above the pub for $90 a week. Can't beat that. The Publican tells me to come back when I'm moving in.

'This isn't the Hilton, we don't take bookings. Turn up

when you want the room. Don't worry, we always have one or two or more.' OK. Cross accommodation off the list.

I cycle back on the main highway. The back way wasn't exactly Beverley Hills 90210. I stop at the Shell Roadhouse where I withdrew the twenty and pick up the local rag and *The Australian* newspaper. Chief reason for this is the racing form guide, but as all lousy punters know, form is temporary, class is permanent. I decide to have a quick look at the beach and it is outstandingly beautiful. Ride back to the Roadhouse and buy a big pouch of roll-your-own tobacco and cigarette papers because I know my own foibles well. It's likely I'll blow the $150 on the GG's and be hanging out for the severance pay on Monday again.

Back at the motel I call my old boss from the pub in Port Hedland and say, 'Andrew, Mr Siddons didn't put my severance pay into my bank account.'

I can hear him smile as he says, 'He's actually coming in on Sunday to do some accounts. I'll get him to put the money into your account overnight Sunday, so maybe Monday, maybe Tuesday.'

'How about definitely...'

'See ya later, Archie.' Bastard hangs up on me. Monday or Tuesday. How about, sorry, money in the account, Monday, no probs. I open the local paper and, geepers, what a splendid form guide they have. All the races: horses, harness and grey-hounds from all over the country. Motel room has an old radio. Cycle back to the Bookie to put the bets on and then come back here and get comfortable and hope they come home. I take a couple of hours over the form and place $100 worth of bets and ride back to the motel. Scratch off the tobacco money and I'm back to the twenty I had in the morning.

It's a nervous day full of anxiety. There's no real pleasure in the events that take place. If I get a winner, it's relief more than joy. I like the roughies, the horses at long odds, but I backed a few favourites as a kind of safety measure and by the end of the day I finish back with the $100 I spent and what now. I ride back into town and pick up the winnings, and at a loose end, I walk into the lounge bar of the pub that has the skimpy girls.

The barman serves me a beer and says, 'There's a topless girl in the public bar.' How odd is that but I can see into the bar and there she is. Maybe only eighteen years old and in her frilly undies and chatting to a bloke about the weather for all I know. She turns to look at me and the thing that hits me; it isn't her breasts or her naked, damp stomach, it's her cold blue eyes and they look straight through me and I leave after my beer.

Sunday is a lay day. I'm extremely tempted to go down to the bookie but the football is on the TV and my impecunious state worries me. I have to get a job. I have to get a job right now, but I'll last two weeks before I have to get unemployment benefits. My team isn't playing in the game but I pick Carlton as the team to barrack for over the despised, Collingwood. Carlton wins in an entertaining game and I pat myself on the back for not gambling.

On Monday the severance pay is in my account and I pay the motel manager, who today is wearing again, the brown slacks and cardigan but with a different colour body shirt. I call a taxi and go to the pub with the $90-a-week rooms and get one. Lock the bike up at the top of the stairwell. The room is small but with a hard single bed and the carpet is in quite good nick. I have a bar fridge and hotplate and there's a very small communal kitchen and a very large, shall I call it, a TV and lounge area, with two couches and multiple armchairs and I wonder how many people live here. The fact that this type of accommodation is becoming standard for me is a worry. I walk to the beach and sunbake for two hours, take a swim, and this is just after winter so the climate is temperate and that makes living easier sometimes.

I read in my room for a few hours. I'm probably behind the times in discovering the young American writer, Nick McDonnell, but I thought his debut book, *Twelve*, was a terrific read and so I'm reading it again, something I often do. Now three hours later I'm just staring into space and the time is 6PM but I've heard no-one coming home from work yet or making any noise in the lounge area. I get up and open my door and walk down the hall into the lounge and the TV is on showing, the 6PM, nightly news. I see some light brown hair hanging over the back of one of the armchairs and come up beside it and walk around it and collapse on the couch and a girl of about 18-20 is sitting and watching the TV.

'Hi,' I say, and she turns and looks at me with cold blue eyes and smiles and I think...*OH, yeah.*

She says, 'Hi.' She's wearing old black jeans and a blue T-shirt and she has these cool, deep blue, Nike trainers on her feet.

'I'm Archie,' I say.

'Where's Sabrina?' she says, and I don't know what she's talking about and then, duh, I go back to the teasing of my school days and...

'Do you read those crap comics?' I ask.

She looks at me and laughs and asks, 'How old are you?'

'Twenty-seven.' Nothing more gets said until the sport comes on and I talk aloud to myself about the cricket score and she ignores me and then the weather guy says it's going to be beautiful in Perth for the whole week but I'm a thousand KMs to the north of the Western Australian capital but the map comes up and shows me the next four days are going to be 25 degrees and sunny every day and the girl turns to me.

'My name is, Kelly Landry, you didn't ask.'

'Oh, sorry, the cricket was on and...'

'Don't worry,' she says and then adds, 'Have you read *Norwegian Wood* by Haruki Murakami?' And my mouth drops open because it's the last thing in the world I thought she was going to say. I usually don't talk about my reading in this type of accommodation because I get short shrift and also I've exposed myself to her as a God-awful snob. And she'll be thinking, *oh yeah this arsehole wouldn't think a girl who works as a skimpy could read anything, let alone Murakami*, and she'd be dead right. But of course, Murakami is hugely popular, just not upstairs at the pub in $90-a-week accommodation in Geraldton, that's all. Not until now anyway. I need to save face somehow.

She says, 'From your reaction, I know you have read it. Don't worry; I know you saw me on Saturday night at work. Do you know my favourite part of that whole book is when Midori gets angry with Toru because he didn't notice her haircut?'

I nod my head and say, 'Have you read his other books?'

'Just *Dance Dance Dance*; and *After Dark*. Do you have a favourite?'

'How come you asked me about Murakami and not someone else?'

'They're my favourite books at the moment. I obsessed about J D Salinger for a while and, oh yeah, I went through a Kerouac phase, and I carried *One Flew Over the Cuckoos Nest* around with me for about a year too, so, at the moment it's Murakami, and you looked like a reader, you know, you just had that look.'

'How old are you?'

'Twenty-two, and I have to go to work now; you can come and talk to me there if it doesn't embarrass you.'

And she looks at me with a big smile on her face that seems to light up her whole body except for those cold blue eyes and I say, 'Maybe not,' and, 'What time do you get up in the morning? Come to the beach with me, tomorrow.'

'I'll knock on your door. You do know we're the only two people living here.' I shake my head and she gets up and picks up her bag and walks out and down the stairs past my bike.

I watch a soap opera on channel 7 and smoke continuously. Walk to the supermarket and buy some gnocchi and pasta sauce; cook and eat with the plate on my lap thinking about Kelly Landry liking Murakami and carrying *One Flew Over the Cuckoo's Nest* around with her for a year and wonder if she might have been teasing me. I go to my room and think about her breasts and her stomach, and after a while I fall asleep.

In the morning she's knocking on my door at 9.45AM and I yell out, 'Just give me fifteen minutes to have a shower.'

'Just take a swim at the beach,' she yells back and it somehow feels like we've been friends forever and when I open the door she smiles and says, 'Come on, slow coach.'

At the beach we sit down and I ask her what's in her bag.

'A full coke bottle of ice, it'll melt; my ciggies; spare undies; a copy of *The Riders* and...'

'No Murakami.'

'Let me finish, would you, and we can talk about him later. My MP3 loaded with great music and a hand towel; three lighters; a box of matches; lip balm; a bathing cap; my purse—but I won't tell you what's in that and—that's it.'

'You like detail.'

She huffs and says nothing more.

I take off my shirt and cut-off jeans and sit in my board shorts, apply a little sun cream. Kelly Landry's wearing a blue bikini, just a plain old blue bikini, and she has the MP3 plugged into her ears. I turn back to look at her ten minutes later and she's taken off the bra, and I stare openly at her breasts and watch the sweat gathered in her stomach, and in that instant she turns over onto her back and the word *perseverance*, in italics, is tattooed on her right shoulder.

She asks me out of the corner of her mouth, 'Did you care about Eri Asai when you read, *After Dark*? I mean it was very interesting her sleeping and all that but I didn't care a thing about her. Let her sleep, I thought.' And she laughs and sits up and says, 'Mari was great though, and Kaoru, the ex-wrestler. I could just keep reading about Mari over and over.'

'I know what you mean about Eri. The first time I read it I thought it was great, the whole thing, everything about the book, but the second time around I skipped over most of that stuff about when Eri was sleeping. Do you want to come for a swim?'

'Yeah, but you can't laugh because I'm going to wear my bathing cap.' And she puts on this ridiculous aqua-coloured bathing cap and my heart melts when she walks down the beach beside me. Just as we're about to reach the water, she takes my hand and says, 'We'll dive under the waves together. After we get to the edge of the water we have to dive under the fifth wave, alright?'

And we do but I break away from her and swim straight out with my head down not looking at where I'm going and I churn through the small surf and stretch out a little faster when I reach the flat water and when I stop and look up, I have to tread water because it's so deep. Kelly is floating on her back fifty metres back toward the beach.

I start to swim back and she stands up and waves to me and then turns and walks back to our laid-out towels. I follow behind her and flop down on my towel and ask her, 'How long are you here for?'

'Probably another four or five weeks. They like to rotate the girls at the pub so the customers don't get bored.'

'What do you usually do?'

'Work in skimpy bars,' she says, looking at me with those cold blue eyes and I turn red with shame. What an arsehole I am. What a snob when I have no reason to be. Me, unemployed and doing nothing.

'It's alright,' she says, 'I know you didn't mean to be malicious.' What a juicy word malicious is and how great it sounds when she says it. She gets her MP3 out of her bag and tells me to come close and sticks the headphones over me and says, 'Close your eyes.'

A sweet sound starts and then the singer invites us to 'Come on...come on', and it's gorgeous. I've never heard it before, 'High above the clouds on a silver line...Come on.' I listen to the whole song and open my eyes.

'Well?'

'Who is it?'

'78 Saab.'

'Never heard of them,' I say.

'You'll hear that song five years from now,' she says, 'and you'll think of this little moment. This perfect day we spent on the beach at Geraldton.' We swim again and laugh and talk of Takahashi, Kaoru, Eri and Mari and *Norwegian Wood* with gorgeous Midori, and she thinks *Franny & Zooey* is better than *The Catcher in the Rye*. She makes a good argument too.

Back at the hotel we lie down on my single bed and she takes her top off and we kiss and she won't allow any more, and we kiss for hours and listen to music and I give her my copy of, *Twelve*.

At 6.30PM she goes to work and tells me to come in and talk to her. At 7.30, I walk down through the main drag of Geraldton, through the mall and back one street to the pub where she works. When I walk in she smiles and says hello really loudly and the manager looks at me. I take a seat at the bar and she draws a beer from the tap for me. It's ice cold and there's only two other people at the bar and it feels awkward but we can talk. Then five guys, all round forty years old, come in, and they're drunk and they hoot and holler a bit and the remarks come out, loud at first, 'great tits', 'nice arse', and then whispered among them like schoolboys and I try to catch Kelly's eye but she's working and she makes every effort to get on with these guys who'll probably leave her tips. She seems to like the attention, and I slink out and go home and read the torn copy of Tim Winton's *'The Riders'* she gave me and fall asleep.

The next morning I walk down the hall to her room and a woman is tearing the sheets of the bed and I ask where Kelly is.

'Left an hour ago,' she says and she sees the look on my face and says, 'Looks like she broke your heart, mister.'

I'll hear that song five years from now and I'll think of that perfect day on the beach at Geraldton.

SID & NANCY

I'd driven up from Melbourne, straight through, petrol stops only, ten hours by the time I got through the city. Bondi.

'Are you tired?' Addy said. I lied and said I wasn't.

'That's great. I've organised with Alicia and her new boyfriend to go and see Beatfish at Salinas. Liandra and Spacy are coming too.'

'What's Beatfish?'

'Martin Plaza from Mental as Anything and James Freud, they started a new band called Beatfish.'

'You would have been about ten when the Mentals were big. Who or what put you...'

'James Freud, babe. That's why. James Freud.'

'Same deal. You would have been about ten when the Models were big. Teenage Radio Stars, you would have been in nappies.'

'Don't get jealous and don't feed me that, 'I was there when' crap. James Freud is hot.'

'He's fucking gay is what he is.' Suddenly I'm very tired.

The last gig I went to at Salinas was Rose Tattoo. Blew my fucking head off. I was wary all night that I might get glassed. How Rock n' Roll is that! Not very. I also saw Radio Birdman (because they are legend) a couple of weeks before the Tatts gig. Wish I hadn't. I was trying to pretend to this girl I just met how 'indie cool' I was. I might have been for about two minutes 15 years ago, but I also remember dancing very badly to Human League, Howard Jones, Flock of Seagulls, and, of course, George 'Freedom 90' Michael. Oh yeah, very cool.

Addy had my number, she knew what I was but she did indulge me on occasions, let me tell her about when I saw the Sunny Boys at Macy's in Melbourne. Great gig by the way. I'm a happy man when I think about that gig.

I'm a little shambolic at the moment. Addy and I had a big blow-up. I took off back to Melbourne without telling her. She freaked out for a couple of days, then tracked me down at Gordon's place.

'Don't tell me your back into the drugs, you stupid bloody idiot.' That's what she said. Assumed it because I was at Gordon's. I did lay down a few lines, well a few; it's all relative, isn't it. To her credit though, she just told me to come back, all was forgiven. I slept (pathetic euphemism) with her best friend, Toya. Best friend no more. I'm just an old sleazebag. Thirty-five's not old but it is because Addy's twenty-one. Sometimes I just think, what the hell, I know it can only last another year, two max, but what else have I got? Addy's amazing, total babe, a firebrand, all constant energy, social wonder woman, everyone loves her, no-one can understand, with the possible exception of Alicia (my old true friend who has been taking Addy's side lately), why on earth she stays with me. I am in capital letters, a dropkick.

. . .

'Alicia made a bet with me that you wouldn't come,' Addy says. 'She reckoned you'd say you were too tired, couldn't be bothered, you go and have a blast though. That's what she said you'd say exactly, 'You go and have a blast.''

'Well, she was wrong, wasn't she? Bloody Alicia, she thinks she knows me back-to-front. She doesn't know shit and if I wasn't such a loyal friend I'd dish the dirt on her, make no...'

'Oh, leave her alone, she loves you for all the right reasons, she's a great friend to you.'

'Are we going out to eat somewhere first or are they meeting us here or what?'

'Or what! You sound so rude sometimes. They're coming here, all four of them, then we're going to the Tratt to eat. Your favourite waitress might serve us,' she says laughing.

'Who...oh, that one in the mornings who always has a hangover. Hey, she's honest at least, and the people who eat there really like her, she plays up the hangovers and gets a few laughs, keeps people happy.'

'Keeps *you* happy. I've seen you checking out her arse.' That's true, she has a great arse and I have been checking it out. Addy says I have a strange obsession with arse, she thinks I might have been gay in a past life. She told me I'd have to pretty much tie her up to get that.

So now the night's laid out for me and I feel like I can manage it. Martin Plaza and Freud. Seems like a strange combo at first but you have to remember it was Freud who sold out, turned the Models into a pop group, the Mentals were always pretty commercial other than the fact that the O'Dougherty brothers looked like they should be selling the 'Big Issue'. What was all that Reg Mombassa shit? He did well though, pretty much made Mambo a household name. Alicia, I wonder if she's going to lay down the law. Tell me I don't know how good I've got it. What I've got is to get my own sorry arse into gear and get some work. I quit the cafe I was working in on Oxford St when I took off back to Melbourne. I had a feeling they were going to sack me anyway, as I made a big fuss about getting paid shift penalties on the weekend. They paid us all cash-in-hand so the other workers got pissed off with me too because they were all on the dole or at uni and getting some sort of Government payment. Will I try the café scene again, maybe here in Bondi; maybe that waitress can get me a job at the Tratt. Better leave that for another day.

'C'mon, Micky, let's have a few drinks before they get here. I bought some Coronas for you and I didn't even cut up lemons cos I know you think that's bullshit. Just drink the beer right!' she says, doing a fair imitation of me. I've been trying to get her to stop calling me Micky. I mean a thirty-five-year-old male shouldn't be called Micky. Michael or even Mike would be better, but I was Micky two years ago when I met her so I'm Micky now. Dropkick.

You're probably wondering how I got her in the first place. I had a book published when I was twenty-three, a novel about a burnt-out rock singer who makes a comeback at thirty-five and burns himself out for a second time only to be saved by the love of a good woman. The book was called *Falling Star*, and I sold about thirty thousand copies and thought I was heading to the freaking top. I was going to...but I didn't. I couldn't get anything published after that. I wrote a big seventy-thousand-word literary novel about a washed-up writer, kind of *Falling Star* for the literary scene. No-one would look at it twice and I gave up. Dropkick. But *Falling Star* was Addy's favourite book and you've worked it all out.

Alicia rocks up about half-an-hour later and introduces us to Steve, who's about my age, I reckon, a couple of years older than Alicia. See that, Steve, not Stevie. He's Mr. Smooth, Alicia's usual fare. Tall, a mess of wavy black hair, good looking like one of those brothers from Spandau Ballet is good looking. Handshake's a little soft for my liking and he kisses Addy on the cheek. They didn't bring anything to drink and we only have four beers left so Steve offers to go to the bottle shop; Alicia hands him a fifty-dollar bill. Keep the change, goes through my mind, and then she corners me while Addy goes into the bedroom.

'You're back in one piece; didn't cut loose in Melbourne, return to those nasty habits of yours.'

'Speaking of which, Alicia, how are you situated for...'

'Easy tiger, just some grass. I'll roll, shall I?'

'You're a disappointment to me, Alicia.'

'Oh Jesus, Micky! When are you going to grow up? You almost blew it here. What do you want from people, from Addy? Grow...up...stupid. And write something, you can't do anything else, write, just sit down and write.'

'You started in early on that one. Write what? I have no ideas.'

'Write your pathetic life story; no-one could believe how many times you've screwed up.' That's the end of the lecture and she sits down and starts to roll a joint and we're best buddies again. All forgiving Alicia. God love her. Only Liandra and Spacy to briefly chastise me now and we're all set to go out. The knock on the door and they're here. Smiles all around and they don't mention my trip to Melbourne. They're Addy's friends and her age and well, they're good people but I can't be alone with just them and Addy and me. Spacy works for Channel Ten, in advertising, and he's the least spacy person I know. Liandra just is. Works with Addy in publishing, doing whatever they do. Not publishing me. We go to the Tratt, eat, no hangover waitress serves us, jump in a taxi to Salinas. Nothing should go wrong tonight, just go with the flow, Mike.

In the taxi, Alicia leans over and whispers in my ear, 'Don't be a saboteur tonight, please.' Point taken.

Salinas is a huge beer barn. Sydney has crap venues compared to Melbourne with the exceptions being The Annandale and Kardomah Café (Bayswater Rd, in the Cross) or whatever it's called this week. We still have an hour before Beatfish are due to hit the stage, and already it's packed, which I'm having difficulty understanding; these guys heyday was ions ago. I look around and understand, Addy, Liandra and Spacy are amongst the youngest here. What we have is a bunch of over-thirties trying to reclaim the night. I offer to buy the first round, which shocks them all, and make my way to the bar. A skinny guy, dressed all in black with dyed black hair, darts in front of me and places his order.

He turns to me and says, 'The Models or the Mentals?'

'Teenage Radio Stars.'

'Are you fucking serious?'

'You wouldn't believe how serious I am,' I tell him.

'I know this guy who played guitar with the Models, he's like a session muso.'

'Here tonight is he or did he grow out of it?'

'What is your problem man?' he says and collects his drinks and moves off. I grab our drinks and turn around and the gang are right behind me. I hand out the drinks and we move as close to the front as possible.

Beatfish kick off with Thin Lizzy's 'The Boys are Back in Town,' but they've turned it into a jangly pop song and it is torture. When the song finishes, I turn to Alicia and say too loudly,

'What the fuck was that?' She gives me a look and shakes her head.

A girl just behind my right shoulder says, 'And who the fuck are you?'

I decide against a reply and James Freud does an intro thing about the band. He's so gay. I know he's married but he's got this whole feline thing going on, all loose wrists and cat prowl, but looking around just confirms what I already knew, the girls love him, the straight guys don't. I'm jealous and I also think back many years ago to seeing The Mentals play in some ballroom in Carlton. Everything was ballroom in those days. Anyway, this girl asked me who I'd like to look like, to be cool you know, and I said Martin Plaza and now I'm still jealous but think the music stinks.

I take in a few songs, get bored and go for a wander around. I run into the skinny guy, dressed in black, from the bar earlier, and we just start talking and he gestures for me to come over next to the bar. I don't apologise, nothing to apologise for, but my demeanour has changed and he can tell I'm in friendly mode, not that I'm scary. I'm a million miles from scary. I ask him about how he knows the guy from the Models.

'I went to school with him,' he says. 'He's a cool guy and I just kind of fell in with that Seaview Ballroom crowd in Melbourne. I just really dug that whole scene.'

'Then surely you wouldn't have been a Mentals fan?'

'That's the funny thing, isn't it? People can't understand how you can like a certain band whose music is totally different from another band you like. Come on, you must have some *supposed* bad albums in your collection?'

I'm really warming to this guy, he's very chilled out and I say, 'You know what, I would have some so-called shit albums in my collection but I don't have a collection. I keep moving house and leaving a trail of my music behind me. Anyway, wherever I've lived there's always been music from other people. Hey, what's your name anyway?'

'Linton, Linton Taylor.'

'That's an impressive moniker. Who are you here with?'

'I came with the drummer, Mick. But I'm on my own out here in the crowd.'

'Come and join us, my girlfriend and some others, we're at the front.'

'Nah, no thanks. I like it here fine, close to the bar and I can see the band. Listen, there's a party later on, with the guys from the band and a heap of other people, come and see me. I'll wait just here after Beatfish finish their set. Bring your friends and I'll let you know where it is.'

'That's very cool, thanks and I'll let the others know. See ya later, I'll come and see you afterwards.'

I make my way back to the others and Addy and Liandra are dancing together like lesbians, kissing each other and half laughing and grinding, and sexy is the only word for it. Spacy's not present and Alicia and Steve are talking, faces pushed close together. Beatfish are live muzak, very average.

I push in between the laughing Addy and Liandra, grab

Addy around the waist and say, 'What are you doing? That's for me.'

'Oh sure,' she says, 'but you get it all the time, and poor Liandra, Spacy took off with a girl he knows and she's lonely.'

'Let her stay lonely. I just met this guy and he's asked us to a party, he knows the band, so you may get to say hello to your hero, James Freud.'

'Wow, that's cool. How come you spoke to this guy? You're usually such a grumpy bum.'

'I don't know, he came up to me twice. At the bar and, yeah, he just kind of sidled up to me again. He's really alright though, you know me, I don't make friends.'

'That's what I mean.'

The gig winds up, one encore, more asked for out of politeness (that kind of gig) than uproarious delight, that's for sure. Alicia and Steve are going back to his place. Spacy and Liandra left earlier in the night. Addy and I decide that we'll give the party a miss and I can't see Linton Taylor anywhere anyway.

We move with the crowd out to Arden St but decide we'll be waiting forever to get a taxi at that exit and turn around and walk up Coogee Bay Rd hoping to get a taxi on its way to Salinas. An old red Mercedes pulls up beside us just as we're almost past the little shopping strip.

Linton Taylor opens the drivers' side door. 'Hey, Mike, are you coming, sorry, I lost you in there, man.' I don't remember telling him my name. The passenger side window lowers and a young girl, maybe eighteen, looks out at us. Her hair is lank and dirty. She hangs her arm out the window and it's pock-marked with scabs that she scratches at, leering at us.

'Jump in the back, it's open,' Linton says. Addy squeezes my hand and I give her a look to say it's okay. The young girl smiles at us and her face transforms into an angel and we climb into the back seat.

The old Mercedes takes off up Coogee Bay Rd with Massive Attack playing gently through the speakers.

'I figured out who you are,' Linton says. '*Falling Star*, you're Michael Anderson.'

'I don't remember telling you my name.'

'Oh yeah, *Falling Star*,' says the young girl and they both start laughing. Addy squeezes my hand again, but I don't look at her. I want to know where this ride is taking us.

'Where's the party?' I ask.

The girl answers slowly and softly. 'The party's later; we're going to a club first. Kind of like the Hellfire Club, only more, hardcore.' The Hellfire Club's gimmick is B&D. Addy went one night and said it was a bit pathetic. Lots of people dressed in leather with the bum cut out, soft whippings. More hardcore, she reckons.

'What's your name? Where's the club at?' Addy asks.

'I'm Nancy and this is Sid,' she says, looking at Linton again and they both laugh. Linton tells us the club is in Erskineville and pops Massive Attack out of the cassette deck.

He searches for a tape, finds it, puts it in the deck, turns around to both of us and says, 'Let's get this fucking party started!' And he looks nothing like the guy I met in Salinas. The opening chords to the Rolling Stones 'Sympathy for the Devil' play out, he turns the volume right up.

I want to see where this ride takes me.

AMERICAN DINER

Lee unfolds *The Age,* reads the headline on the front page, then goes straight to the back page of the business section to sport. His strong latte gets placed in front of him.

'Thanks Ahmed, this is great.' Lee pays him exactly $3.05 because sometimes he forgets to pay and just walks out.

He smiles up at Ahmed, who says, 'How about something to eat? A big breakfast, a burger, some bread and dip? You can't survive on coffee.'

'Um, I can't really afford it.'

'Ten-dollar breakfast. Eggs on toast, bacon, mushrooms, lettuce and tomato. Any sauce you want. Be a big spender.'

Lee is a singer/songwriter who isn't getting many gigs lately, which is something he can't work out. He doesn't usually have breakfast until about midday, after the first joint, and he cooks at home. He works part-time delivering pizzas. Can't afford even the $10 special but that's about to change courtesy of an expected benefactor.

Lee shrugs his shoulders, says, 'Hey, Ahmed, have you ever

been to America and eaten in one of those diners over there? I hear you can get these massive meals for like three or four dollars and an endless cup of coffee.'

'You want a four-dollar breakfast. Go. Go to America. This café isn't good enough for you.'

'No, man. I didn't mean it like that. I mean, you know, you see them in movies and stuff and...' But Ahmed had walked away, cursing Lee.

It's 10AM and Lee lights the first cigarette of the day.

Ella walks in at 10.15AM, tall and gorgeous in black skinny jeans, a black skivvy, wearing short, black, Cuban-heeled boots. Her blond hair cut short, like Andy Warhol's *it girl*, Edie Sedgewick. Huge brown eyes staring at Lee.

'What the? How did you know I was here?'

'I stopped in at the house and Sarah said you'd gone out early so I took a guess.'

'Oh, right.'

'Hey,' she says, 'are you fucking her?'

'What is with you? No, I'm not, She...'

'You tried and failed.'

'Hey, Ella, guess what?'

'Surprise me.'

'I'm finally going to America.'

'Oh yeah, right. On all that money you saved delivering pizzas three nights a week at ten bucks an hour.'

'Oh, you of little faith.'

'You're serious.'

'Yeah. My uncle lent me the money.'

'You never even mentioned you had an uncle.'

'Have you told me about your uncles and aunts?'

'OK. This is getting stupid. Why did he lend you the money?'

'My dad and my uncle had a talk; my dad thinks I'm

wasting my life trying to be a muso and they came up with this scheme. My uncle is a picture framer and he's going to lend me the money on the condition I come back and learn the business. They think I need to get this whole America thing out of my system.'

'How much money?'

'I asked for ten, but he gave me eight.'

'Eight thousand dollars.'

'Yes.'

'When we were going out you said over and over you had no money and now this and OH NO, you're never going to pay him back are you?'

'Of course, I am. I'm going to make it.'

'Of course you are, but if you don't, you'll pay him back in your own special way over about fifty years like all the cash you borrowed off me. You're betraying your dad and your uncle and me too.'

Both of them say nothing for a while until Ahmed comes over and says, 'Hello, pretty lady, you want your cappuccino?'

'Thanks, Ahmed, it's so cool that you remember my coffee preference.'

Ahmed stares at Lee as if to say, *this is how a good customer should be.* And he walks back behind the counter.

Lee says, 'He's got a hard-on for you.'

'Oh, come on. Don't be stupid.'

They both sit and say nothing. Ella stares at Lee wanting to kill him. They had made plans so many times to go overseas together but he never had the money. Ella's working in a Chapel St dress shop as a sales assistant, so she doesn't earn much money, but if her dad lent her money, she'd damn well pay him back. Lee continues to read the sports section.

Ella says, 'You know sometimes when I'm on the tram

going to work. I start thinking about us doing *it,* like when we were going out, and I get so wet I want to touch myself.'

Lee sits back, looks at her, and Ella stretches back and runs her right hand through her short blond hair, smiles at him. Lee says, 'God, Ella, you're the most amazing girl.'

'And you cheated on me, you rat. The pizza boy cheated on me.'

'I thought you forgave me for that.'

'Why did we break up?'

'Because I cheated on you and...'

'And that means I don't forgive you; otherwise, we'd be together. But you know what. If we hadn't broken up, I bet your dad and uncle wouldn't have come up with this scheme because they knew, everybody knew, that I was in love with you and I'm a good person and you would have changed eventually and got your shit together for both of our sakes. So, again, you're in debt to me for...'

'Mike Connors is having a party tonight. One of his fantastic wild parties in that big house on Punt Road. His parents are in France so it should be a wild...'

'A wild night. Shit. I wish I had five dollars for every time you said that. I have to go,' she says just as Ahmed puts down her cappuccino.

'I'm sorry, Ahmed, I have to go, but here,' and she digs into the money pocket of her black skinny jeans and hands him four dollars and says, 'It's OK, a tip for putting up with this idiot.'

Ahmed laughs and Lee smiles in spite of himself. Ahmed says, 'He's a big shot. Going to eat in American diners.'

Walks off shaking his head again.

'You told him?' Ella says.

'Long story.'

'Will you pick me up from work this afternoon?'

'Sure.'

'Hey, when do you leave, Lee?'

'Two days,' he says, and he can see the look of disappointment on her face.

She looks away for a few seconds then says, 'Don't forget, pick me up on Chapel St, we can go and eat together before the party.'

'OK. Hey, I love you,' Lee says.

'Yeah, right,' Ella says not looking back.

Ella hops on the tram at Church Street to go to work. She knows Lee loves her, he just can't keep his dick in his pants. She thinks she might kiss a guy tonight, right in front of Lee. But most probably she won't. Lee should've... It should be his second name, Should've. He's going to take his guitar and songs to try and get gigs in America. She wonders what city he's going to in America first? Where's he first touching down?

Oh, Lee can sing like an angel. She was in the shower one day, not long after she first had sex with him at her place in East Richmond. Lee was in the kitchen singing and playing guitar to that Van Morrison song, 'Brown Eyed Girl'...it was so beautiful. It was the first time she knew she was in love with him. When she got out of the shower she hugged him, told him how beautiful it was.

He said, 'Take it easy, Ella, you're getting water all over my shirt.'

In those first few months, he had a residency at the Armadale Hotel in Malvern and various other gigs around town. He'd sing some Jackson Browne and Van Morrison, of course, and a great version of Fleetwood Mac's, 'Go Your Own Way.' He started singing his own songs, got a good reputation. An A&R guy came to watch him one night.

Ella gets off the tram just as Lee walks out of the café. She remembers Lee being rude to the A&R guy and how when they got home, he said, 'He works for some small Australian label who want to find the next Pseudo *fucking* Echo. He kept asking me if I do *Alt Rock*. I don't even know what that is. He said I had *the right look*. Fuck that shit.'

Ella told him they were the biggest label in Australia, but he just shook his head and said, 'If I had to work with people like that, I'd go insane.'

Ella is positive the A&R guy put the word out to pubs and bars not to hire Lee because Lee was so rude to him. It's the only explanation because Lee was, as they say, on his way.

Then the residency at the pub ended, and he cheated on Ella and she dumped him, and now this.

America.

Ella was having a shit day at work. This woman fishing for compliments when she tried on a dress. Ella lying to her face about how great she looked, then Lee rang, said straight out, 'I want you to come with me to America.'

'What?'

'You heard me. The eight thousand from my uncle is on top of the airline ticket. You have a couple of thousand saved, don't you? I'll pay for your ticket, we'll go together. Put all the shit behind us.'

'Lee, you leave in two days.

'We'll go to Flight Centre and book the ticket as soon as you knock off.'

'What about my job? What about my boss? How will she find a...'

'Stuff her. If the situation was reversed, she'd sack you in a minute without a day's notice.'

'Oh, Lee, it's that attitude. What if you get sick of me? What if I...'

'Come with me, please. I'll be there at five when you knock off. Think about it, babe, you and me in America.'

Ella thinks about Lee after she hangs up. He has the jet-black hair of a rocker, a hard handsome face, and despite the fact he never exercises, a slim, hard body. He told Ella it was from swimming at school, training three or four times a week from when he was eight or nine right up until he finished year 12. That attitude though. Stuff her, he said about her boss. But she wasn't making it up when she told him about how she sometimes felt on the tram. And on stage he was magnetic, the whole crowd drawn to him.

Lee sits around at home, strumming his guitar, writing songs in his head and the phone rings.

'Hello.'

'Hi, Lee, it's Ella.'

'What's up, why'd you ring so quickly?'

'I don't want to go with you, Lee. It's your dream, go ahead, chase it. Take your guitar and songs and go without me.'

'Oh, um, shit, you still haven't forgiven me.'

'It's not that. I mean it is and it isn't. You're so frustrating. You didn't ask me straight away. This is an afterthought. You think if things go screwy in America, you'll still have me.'

'No, no. That's not it.'

'Look, I'm going to my mum's house after work. I don't want to go to the party. I don't want to see you before you go.' Lee doesn't say anything, the beats click over, Ella says, 'Bye, Lee.'

'Ella, wait!'

'What?'

'Meet me one more time, tomorrow, back at the café.'

'OK, tomorrow at 11AM. '

'Thanks, Ella, bye.'

The next day Lee is back at the café near the corner of Swan and Church St in Richmond. Ahmed isn't there. Lee has a hangover from the party and is starving. Ella was coming to meet him soon. His uncle had put the money into his bank account, so he was eating a big greasy hamburger with the lot.

Ella walked in wearing all black again. Sat opposite him, said, 'This better be good. What's so important?'

'Ella, if I don't make it as a singer or even as a songwriter for some crummy label, would you still love me? I mean, could you go out with, maybe live with a picture framer? Would it be so bad?'

Ella shakes her head, says, 'You know *Diner,* that film you love so much. About those guys in their mid to late twenties meeting up at their favourite diner and shooting the breeze like it's the greatest thing on earth.'

'Yeah, I know what it's about. Shit.'

'But if it was you, Lee, you'd be sitting there on your own. No room for anyone else. None of us meet your great standards. We're not cool enough. Here you are two days in a row. You arrived on our own and you'll leave on your own. None of us are good enough for you. I'm a backup plan if things fail.'

Lee shakes his head, says, 'Come home with me now.'

'Aah, shit, Lee, no.'

'Come on. You want to.'

'No.'

THE SUN BATHER

I arrived in Sydney three days ago. I just up and moved my life here. Once I decided it was relatively easy. I came from Melbourne. I don't know anyone who lives here. I always liked the idea that Sydney had surf beaches in the city: Bondi, Tamarama, Bronte, Coogee, and Maroubra. I don't surf. I body surf. I'm in a motel in Curlewis St, Bondi. I've been in the surf every day of the three days. I've been checking out the papers on a daily basis for work. I arrived on a Saturday. It's December 1988. I'm twenty-five.

I moved to Coogee to cheaper accommodation; a room with a bed and sofa, a little bathroom and a small kitchen. I bought a TV and video. I walked from Bondi to Coogee to check it out and I thought at the time I could just keep walking, walk for years, like Harry Dean Stanton in Paris, Texas. I've always had that feeling that I could just up and walk and keep on walking.

The small flat or studio apartment or flatette, whatever you choose to call it, is in a block of flats on Dolphin St very close to the beach. Maybe a 3-to-5-minute walk. No view. Today is

Friday morning and I walk from the flat to Coogee Bay Rd and find a café. I sit down and this girl, the waitress, she's wearing this bright lemon-coloured dress, more like something you'd see at a fashion show or so it looks to me.

She wears it like it's no big deal. I get dressed up like this every day, so who cares, and she says to me, 'Hello, corfee?' Like that, corfee, not coffee. I almost laugh and she smiles and says, 'I live in the same block as you. I saw you move in yesterday. Do you like the place? I hate it but I'm not moving.'

'Oh, you hate it, huh? Yeah, coffee, a latté. Can I have two poached eggs on toast too?'

'Sure.' She has these really thick dark eyebrows but her hair is blond, and this sounds weird, but I can't work out whether she dyed her eyebrows or her hair and it makes me smile. Her hair is tied up with two wispy strands hanging down on either side. You can tell she did this on purpose. A look she likes. She has black Dunlop Volleys on her feet. I told you about the lemon dress. I'm one of about eight people in the café that seats about twice as many as that.

'I'll bring the corfee,' she says and walks off and I wonder which flat is hers. Does she have a boyfriend? Does he live with her?

I pretend to read the *Sydney Morning Herald* but all the time I'm watching her. She brings the coffee and I ask her, 'What's your name?'

'Rhoda,' she says. 'I can't talk much here; the boss is a grouch.' And I look up to see a big beefy woman at the espresso machine, looking rather unkindly at us.

'No problem,' I say and drink my latté and read the paper. The big beefy woman delivers the eggs.

I don't see Rhoda until I start to walk out when she takes my arm and says, 'I'll come and visit you. A welcome drink, alright?'

I nod and she turns away and I watch her move through the café and I go home and sit and mope a little and then I put my board shorts and a T-shirt on and swim at Coogee and I joke to myself that Coogee must be an Aboriginal word for seaweed because there's so bloody much of it. But the water is lovely, beautiful. There's no real surf close to the beach. Wedding Cake Island sits off the beach waiting for a party to happen, and I hope that Rhoda brings that drink this evening. I look up and see a young blond girl lay out her towel and then sit down. She takes a bottle of suntan oil out of her bag. She's wearing a blue bikini bottom and a red top that she immediately takes off. She puts some oil on her legs and rubs it in, applies some to her stomach and her breasts. I'm rushing telling you about it, but she does everything slowly. I'm fixated on her for half-an-hour as the day gets hotter and hotter and she turns onto her stomach. I get up and leave.

Rhoda doesn't come around, and the next morning I'm too self-conscious to go to her café, so I waste my money at a smaller café on Dolphin St. I have the employment section and I go through the general vacancies. That's me, a 'general hand'. No qualifications unless you count year 12 secondary school. People, prospective employers are always asking, 'Did you finish secondary school?' I hate it even though I have it. I feel like screaming, I'm going for a job as a hotel porter what possible difference could it make, and that's where I finish up on Tuesday morning. At an interview I don't want to be at. I get the job and he tells me to start the following Monday. I call him back and say, 'No thanks.'

The next day the landlord knocks on my door. It's not rent day and he says, 'Ivan, you want some work?'

'Doing what?'

'I have six vacant flats. You can paint them, slowly. Do three hours a day for me. I can't pay you, but you get your rent for free. There are fifteen flats, including this one. You'll eventually do them all. I have other properties, some gardening work.' I don't say anything.

'Yes, no. You can't work three hours a day?'

'Yes, yes. I'll do it.'

'Tomorrow. 9AM. We start. OK?'

'OK.'

The next morning, I look for the rooms to be painted. I go up to the third floor and a door opens at the end of the hall and Rhoda walks out with this tall guy, who has black, very short hair. I keep walking towards her. She's wearing a high-waisted, pleated red skirt with a white sleeveless shirt. She cut her hair. It's short but has no style, it looks like it's been hacked off with a pair of blunt scissors but somehow it makes her look better. She's wearing these thick, high heeled, brown shoes. It makes her taller than me. The guy is wearing blue jeans and a blue denim jacket. She's embarrassed to see me, and I don't know what to say.

The landlord, Thomas, pops his head out of the room on the opposite side and says, 'C'mon, work to do. Look at Rhoda, always a new boyfriend.'

And everyone stops and the guy smiles and keeps walking along the hall, and Rhoda stops and lets him go like she's embarrassed to be seen with him. At the end of the hall, he stops and turns and Rhoda turns and goes back into the room. The guy shrugs and walks away. I say hi to Thomas and he says, 'Alright, Mr. Ivan. You have the paint. So paint. Three hours, no more, every day. Two coats, please.' I shrug and smile; Thomas is just one of those guys people like. I can tell life isn't too serious for Thomas, but still he's got these flats and others so he must be pretty smart or maybe he just inherited it all.

I paint for an hour, stop, light a smoke. Three hours can be actually painting for three hours. I can take as many breaks as I like. At least that's what I'm telling myself. I start again and five minutes later there's a tapping on the open door. Rhoda with two mugs of coffee, one in each hand, looking like she should be on the catwalk in that red, pleated skirt.

'Take a break, Ivan. I have corfee.' I like the sound of my name in her mouth. I stop.

'Here,' she holds out the coffee.

I take it and say, 'Don't be embarrassed about before.'

'Oh, I'm not. He, ah, doesn't matter.'

'Why?'

'Oh, he wouldn't stop talking about himself. It's good if guys can talk and I don't mind normally, he just, I...it was boring.'

'How do you make a mistake like that?' I ask and she shrugs.

'Thomas must like you.'

'Yeah, maybe. Can I talk about myself?'

She laughs and says, 'I'll tell you if you're boring. I couldn't go through that again so quickly.'

'No, it's just, um. I have some money saved and I'm getting unemployment and now free rent for doing this (I wave my arms around) three hours a day and he says he has some more work. It's a little like a paid holiday. I can go to the beach and it takes that pressure off. You know, to *be* somebody. So, when people ask me, what do you do? I can say back to them. I just moved here from Melbourne and I'm taking things slowly.'

'Anything else you want me to know?'

'How come you dress like a model? You live here, which isn't what you'd call upmarket, but you dress...'

'I make my own clothes. It's really not that difficult.'

'Is that what you want to be? A designer or to work in fashion'

'No. I just like doing it. Maybe I'm a bit like you. I don't want to *be* anything.'

She looks at me and I don't say anything, and she keeps looking, a little smile comes to her face. I say, 'You cut your own hair too.'

'You noticed.'

'You never came around with that welcome drink.'

'No. I will I promise. Don't believe what that awful Thomas said. It's never more than two boys in one week.' And she can tell she rocked me and I look away and she laughs and picks up the two coffee cups and turns and goes back into her flat.

When I've done my three hours, I knock on Rhoda's door but she doesn't answer. Maybe she sneaked out while I was painting. I leave the door and windows open and amble back to my room. I'm reading and someone knocks on the door. I answer and it's Thomas.

'Here,' he says, 'I wrote down the flat numbers. Take your time.'

'Alright,' I say and smile. 'Thanks.'

I walk down to the beach and sunbake for a while. The blonde girl in the blue bikini is back and she's about thirty metres away from me up towards the road. I watch her apply suntan oil all over her body. She's beautiful. The beach isn't crowded. She takes off the red bikini top and applies oil to her breasts, slowly, like a kind of show or something and I have to look away. I get up and go for a swim. The water is cold and it feels wonderful, and I swim out for 200 metres and stop and tread water and look at the people walking along the path and back at the girl who turns over onto her stomach. I swim in and catch a tiny little wave when I'm close to the shore and I walk up the beach. The blond is gone.

Back at the flat I'm watching TV and my door is open.

Rhoda knocks and comes in with a bottle of Champagne. Holds it up like a trophy.

'Hi,' she says.

'That welcome drink.' I say.

'Should I christen the place like a boat and shake the bottle up and pop the cork?'

'I'd rather drink it.'

'Me too,' she says and unwraps the silver paper off the top and gently pops the cork and says, 'Glasses or cups or something.'

'Close the door.' I say and she does. I get two mugs from the kitchen. She pours beautifully and I take in what she's wearing. It's like a 1950s dress, something you might wear to a party. It has thick red shoulder straps and the hem is just below the knee. The main part of the dress is light blue and has small red, rectangle shapes on it and it has like a cummerbund, a thick red belt, and she wears red flat shoes.

I sip and ask, 'Another one of your creations?' Clearly I know nothing of fashion.

'Oh, this old thing,' she says and laughs and sits on my two seater sofa and smiles a shy smile and we talk about films and books, and when the champagne is finished, she invites me to the premiere of this new film that's coming out.

I ask her, 'How did you get tickets for it?'

And she says, 'Oh, my mum is a big wig. She knows people.' I look at her like she's mad and she says, 'Don't worry, you'll get used to me. Be ready at 6PM tomorrow, we'll catch a taxi to the city.' And she's gone and my life is empty again and I go to sleep and dream of the sunbather girl on the beach and Rhoda in my bed.

I do my painting and don't see Rhoda. I think about why I came to Sydney. Sick of Melbourne, I told everyone when I left, and it wasn't really any more than that. I was just bored. I had a relationship, but it was boring and I couldn't see any way out of it, same with the job I had. I was a clerk in a transport company and your work so defines you, and in Melbourne it matters where you went to school. Last night Rhoda said that in Melbourne people always ask you where you went to school and in Sydney it's where you live. I just got sick of apologising for my job. My girlfriend kept telling me how intelligent I was and how I could do so much better.

I think I'd like to have a job at a cinema or in a library or perhaps to write screenplays or books; that's why I was so shocked when Shelley said she has these tickets. Connections, I thought. I have no idea where to start. I try to think of the last Australian film I saw. I think it was *My First Wife*, starring Wendy Hughes and John Hargreaves, and I thought at the time that it was brilliant, but honestly no-one went to see it. It had hardly opened before it closed.

I go to the beach again and the blond girl walks onto the sand into the same spot she was yesterday. I prepare myself for the show and she doesn't let me down. She does it so slowly, so luxuriously, so languid, I'm mesmerised. I wait until she turns onto her stomach and go and swim again and watch her from the ocean. She stays another hour and I watch her leave and she walks towards the Coogee Bay Hotel.

What the hell will I wear to this film tonight? I don't even know what male fashion is. It's nearly thirty-five degrees; it'll still be very hot at six when she comes to get me. I have a job interview suit, but I won't wear it. Jeans and a T. Scruffily cool, I lie to myself, but it's bugging me.

Rhoda knocks on the door and says, 'C'mon, we'll get the bus, no need to waste money on a taxi.' Her hair is slicked down on her scalp with hair cream or something, with a side part. I think she looks like that skinny model from the sixties, Twiggy. The clothes are sixties too. Her dress is powder blue and clinched at the waist and then it billows out. She looks absolutely sensational.

I say, 'You look amazing.'

She shrugs and says, 'C'mon, let's go.'

On the bus I say, 'I'm sorry about the old jeans and T, but it's so hot and I really have no idea what fashion is, what I should wear to a film premiere.'

She looks surprised and says, 'For God's sake, don't worry. You can get it up, can't you? That's the only prerequisite for a date with me.' And we both burst out laughing and I'm relieved and she says, 'What's the sound of summer this year?'

'You mean like a song, a standout summer track?' I ask.

'That's what DJs say. The sound of summer this year is... and what is it? Tell me. I haven't listened to the radio for weeks.'

'Could be that English singer, Rick Astley, ah, what's that song called? Um, 'Never Gonna Give You Up.' I think it's putrid, but it could be the answer.

She looks perturbed and says, 'No silly, your song, what's your summer song of 1988, nearly, 1989.'

'I have to say 'Kokomo' by the Beach Boys. Can't get any more summer than that and it's the theme to that movie, *Cocktail*, with Tom Cruise. And what's this film we're seeing, you haven't told me.'

'*Colours.*'

'Oh, I've heard of that. Sean Penn is in it.'

'Yeah, it's about gangs in LA.' We sit quietly for the rest of the trip and get off the bus opposite Hyde Park. The film starts at 7.30; we have forty-five minutes. We walk across to the park; the cinema is in George St; we sit on a bench and smoke.

After the film we sit on the 373 bus in the second to back seat and hold hands. Rhoda looks out the window and then turns to me and says, 'Stay with me, tonight.'

I nod and ask, 'Who was the guy I saw you with? The first day I started the painting.'

'Oh, nobody. I told you. Just some boring guy I'll probably never see again.' I shrug but it annoys me.

At the flats, she opens her door and turns and puts her arms around my neck and says, 'You're really sweet. I knew it that first day I saw you. You're gentle. In the café, you were nice too. You have good manners.' And we kiss and then she takes my hand and leads me to the bed. I sit and she sits in my lap and we fall back and kiss again and our hands grab at each other, stripping off our clothes. I wake up at 3AM and she's awake too and she grinds into me and I get an image of the blond girl on the beach, languidly applying the oil to her body. Rhoda kisses down my stomach and I keep the image of the blond girl in my head, and she keeps kissing down my body and my head swirls with the pleasure of it all.

Afterwards, I tell her about the girl and she giggles and says, 'Oh, I thought it was all me.'

In the morning I wake at 8AM. She's gone and there's a note telling me she's gone to work in the café and help myself to coffee or come into the café. I look around the flat and there's no sewing machine, no material or cloth or anything to do with making clothes. I get out of bed and open her wardrobe and it's full of clothes and shoes. There's a suitcase on the floor of the wardrobe also filled with clothes and another suitcase on the small sofa and I open it and it's full of more clothes and I can't figure it out. I think of what she said in the café on that first day.

'I hate it but I'm not moving.' And tickets to film premieres. How does that work with living in this place with all these clothes that she claims to have made? I'm snooping, and when you snoop, it's like eavesdropping, you only learn bad things. I find a photo of the tall guy in amongst her underwear in the top drawer. I get my clothes together and decide not to paint today.

I walk around the flats trying to find Thomas to tell him I won't be working but can't find him anywhere. I go back to my flat. Last night was great. I put on my board shorts and walk out. At the entrance to the flats, I pass the tall guy whose photo I just saw. I wait. I figure I'll start a conversation with him when he comes back out. I'm still waiting twenty minutes later. He must have a key or he lives here too. Shit. I walk down to the beach and lay out my towel. I listen to my Walkman.

Ten minutes later I look up and see the blond sunbather. She applies the oil again to her long dark legs and stomach and she pours the oil on her breasts, I swear to God she's looking straight at me. I stare at her and she stares right back. I turn away and then back again and she's lying down. After an hour I look back and she's looking again. I stand up and walk towards her and she watches me coming.

I kneel down next to her and say, 'Hi, I'm Ivan.'

'Hi,' she says.

'OK, if I sit down?'

'Um, yeah, sure, I guess.'

'I was thinking about you last night.'

HOMECOMING

'Hi, Linda.'

    'Tesky! Hi!'

    'I'll be in Sydney in a week for four weeks.'

    'You want to know if I'm available,' she says.

'Hey, c'mon, you know it's more than that.'

'For the past four years, you've come home at Christmas and expected me to be your girlfriend for four weeks and then you disappear back up the coast to Ballina and I don't hear from you for another...'

'Oh, come on. I write to you.'

'When you're here you tell me you love me, and when I get a letter it's, oh, we had this huge party and the dope crop is going really well and blah, blah, blah.' And Linda hangs up and Tesky thinks it must be over.

He feels weird. He usually goes home to Sydney by bus and spends two days at Sharon's (his mum) house. She's cool; smokes weed, does Reiki and all that shit. After that he's always gone and spent the rest of the time with Linda, other than going back to Sharon's for three days over Christmas.

117

It's never mattered with Linda before. She never had a go at him like that. Whether she had her own pad or was in share house, she always just said, 'Cool. Come straight over.' She must have a boyfriend. This confuses Tesky. These four weeks are like some kind of grand homecoming each year. Everyone says, you know, hey man, still up north and good to see you, and it feels comfortable. People are glad to see him. He's thirty, so is Linda. They've been friends who sleep together since they were eighteen or nineteen. They'd fall in and out of love and meet other people, and then he came on this house in Ballina. He was on his way to Byron and he stopped in Ballina and on the noticeboard at the library there was this notice for a share house. He called up and he's been there ever since. There are four people in the house. Tim, a quiet man who wants to be a writer; he gets stories and poetry published in small magazines. Two girls: Terri and Sandra. They are the quintessential hippies of all time. They rarely have visitors. Tesky has sex with Sandra and Tim has sex with Terri. Terri and Sandra have sex. Tesky saw the girls having sex once, through a gap in a partially closed door, and he can't get it out of his mind. There is no *ménage a trois*.

They don't have a TV or DVD. They have music from a small stereo, but it's never played loudly. Sandra has a beautiful voice and she plays guitar and sings Joni Mitchell, Joan Baez and Luka Bloom. They have the dope plants on a private farm. The farm belongs to a friend of Terri. The girls let Tesky pick up his own supply by going through the gates in Terri's old Ford. The girls sell the dope in large quantities to a guy who comes down from Byron Bay once every three months. They also have a fairly large quantity of indoor hydroponic plants. Tesky's not in on the deal.

He's roughly explained all this to Linda, leaving out the sex, and telling her the dope is personal use only. He makes up stories about big parties and a lot of other stuff when he writes to her because he thinks his life might sound boring otherwise. Tesky is kind of sad because Sandra doesn't love him. He knows that. She loves Terri and Terri loves her.

He sits in the kitchen of the house in Ballina. The soft lino floor peels upwards. Sun shining through the open window. A hint of breeze blows open the white curtains. A black and white cat squats, lapping at a bowl filled with milk. His burning cigarette sits in a ceramic ashtray. There is a small green Buddha on the windowsill with a burnt-out incense stick stuck in his belly. The brown kettle on the gas ring starts to whistle and Tesky sighs and gets up and takes the kettle off the gas and pours the boiling water onto some instant coffee in a white mug. He sits back down and butts out the cigarette and takes another one from his pack and lights it with a dark blue lighter. Linda hung up on him.

The phone rings and Tesky picks it up and says, 'Hello.'

'Hi, Tesky, I'm sorry I hung up on you yesterday. I was having a bad day. You can stay at my place when you're not at Sharon's, if you still want to.'

Tesky smiles and says, 'Great, that's great.'

There's an awkward silence before Linda says, 'Is there a girl up there, Tesky? You told me about Sandra and Terri. I know they're gay, but is there someone else? Why do you stay up there?'

Tesky tells the truth, 'It's so peaceful. So quiet. I like working only three days a week and I like the work. The rent is so cheap. Everyone in the house respects everyone else.' And then lies, 'There's no girl. Just me.'

'Tesky, are you saying you only have sex for four weeks of the year, with me?'

'No. No. I meant that I'm not in love with anyone else.'

'Good.'

'I have to go to work,' he says and hangs up.

He's not working today. He works in a small canning factory. He's on an assembly line but he likes it. The monotonous routine works for him and it's only five hours a day. He gets his dope for free. They share all the bills. When he says to himself it's not a bad life, he means it.

Linda sits in her own small kitchen in Annandale and thinks she's going to have to shake Tesky up. There's more to life than getting stoned and leading a peaceful existence. She's going to challenge him. She's going to put pressure on him like she never has before. She's going to ask him if he could be anything, what he would be. Linda began making ends meet by doing clothing repairs. She makes her own clothes and other people see her clothes and she makes dresses for them in similar styles. People come to her and describe what they want and she creates these clothes for them. What happened in the past year is that everything started taking off through word of mouth. More and more people wanted her to make clothes for them and she rented a small workplace in Ultimo and also hired a seamstress to work for her. It's a tiny operation but she's making more money than she ever thought she would and the only thing missing is Tesky. She hasn't told him about this important success.

Sandra walks into the kitchen in her light blue harem pants and the sun shines through them to reveal her naked form and Tesky looks at her and sighs. Sandra has short, light brown hair with a rat's tail at the back. She sometimes plaits the rat's tail.

120

She has thick thighs and strong legs. A big firm ass. Her upper body is strong too with small firm breasts. She does yoga and chants.

She looks at Tesky and takes the cigarette out from between his fingers, takes a drag and says, 'I have to stop this foul habit. It consumes me.' But what she does is light the gas ring and put the brown kettle back on the stove and take a cigarette from the pack in front of Tesky and light up and say, 'You like having sex with me don't you.'

'Yes,' Tesky says, a little unsettled.

'Why?'

Tesky looks at her blue-grey eyes and says, 'I like your body. I like what you do to me.'

'Good. Are you going to be staying with Linda in Sydney?'

'Probably, yeah. I don't want to lose her, but I don't want to leave here either.'

'Do you love me or like me and just want the sex?'

'I know you love Terri, not me. I'm not even sure why you have sex with me.'

'You're a chilled-out guy, Tesky. I'm bi and I like you. It's hard not to like someone like you, but if you love this girl, Linda, then you need to give up this life and find out what it is you want to be and who you want to be that person with.'

'I always wanted to create something. I did this course in Sydney on how to make stained glass. You know like the windows in churches. The Signs of the Cross done in stained glass. I was good at it, but I didn't take it any further. You could make a living doing that.'

The kettle boils and Sandra takes the lid off and in an instant changes her mind and turns to Tesky and takes his hand and says, 'Come back to bed.'

In bed a little later, Sandra turns to Tesky and says, 'People have stained glass windows in their homes. In their front doors and lounge rooms and as lampshades. Plus, there are businesses. If you were good at it, there's obviously people who would pay you to do it.'

'Yeah, I'd need to do the course again or a more advanced course to get back the feeling, to get my skills back up but I did really like it. I'd need tools of course and...'

'And you'd have to do the course in Sydney so you could stay with Linda.'

'You don't care if I'm here or not do you?' Tesky says. Sandra doesn't answer him.

The week passes and the night before he's due to leave Tesky calls Linda.

'I sort of thought you might be over me staying with you, that you might want something more serious. Are you sure it's cool for me to...'

'Yeah, I told you. I'm sorry I hung up on you.'

'I might stay in Sydney, it's not one-hundred percent, but I told the others in the house just in case. I'll pay them for two weeks more if I go through with it. I have an idea, uh, I'll talk to you about it when I get there.'

'What brought this on?' Tesky smiles, he's glad about this. A little nervous, sure, but he's glad about it, yeah.

'Time to be someone, maybe, to set a few goals.' She should have hung up on him more often. He still has the safety net of the house in Ballina.

The next day he gets on the bus with his books and music and finds a seat three rows forward from the toilet and puts his backpack on the seat next to him. To be moved only if someone asks to sit there. No-one does. The bus is only half-full. The aircon is on but the driver has it at the right temperature. He's feeling good. Sandra, Terri and Tim wished him well. He knew where they had the course for making stained glass. He did it at Sydney TAFE last time. The campus on Broadway. He hadn't seen it like he's seeing it now. As a future, a career where Linda could say to her friends, he makes stained glass windows. He drifts off to sleep as they pass through Dirty Creek.

He wakes up and puts his headphones on and looks out the window for hundreds of miles not seeing anything. Eight hours later the bus steams into Sydney over the Harbour Bridge at night and he looks at the Opera House and the high-rise buildings and feels nothing. His mother lives in Leichhardt, maybe 10km west of the city and 3kn further west than Annandale and Linda. He grew up in Leichhardt. Knows every café on Norton St and the inside of every pub in Leichhardt and Five Dock. If he could live anywhere, he'd buy a house in the tiny suburb of Summer Hill. That's his Sydney, not the bright shiny world of the harbour, the Opera House and the tall buildings.

The bus pulls into Circular Quay and Tesky eases himself out of the seat. He hasn't said a word to anyone the whole trip. He walks to the bus stop, and in five minutes he's on the L38 express bus to Leichhardt. He calls Linda.

'Tesky, you made it.'

'Yeah, I... I thought I might stay with you, straight away, see Sharon tomorrow, is that OK? Let me know, quick, cos the bus is near your stop.'

And he half–laughs when he says it and Linda laughs and says, 'Get off, stupid.'

'OK.' He presses end on his cell phone. A minute later he gets off and walks down Johnston St smiling. Turns right into Collins and then left at Wells St. He hasn't been here before; she was living in Leichhardt last time, not far from Sharon. Number 15 is a house, a tiny weatherboard house, and he knocks on the door and Linda opens it almost straight away and grabs him by the T-shirt and kisses him hard on the mouth.

He kisses her back and breaks away and says, 'Let me get inside, Jesus.' She lets him in and takes his hand and leads him through the house past the lounge room, the bathroom, her bedroom, and into the kitchen. The outside light is on and he can see out the back window onto a small cement courtyard that has tree ferns planted around it in black soil and a tiny tin shed. The kitchen is the same as the one in Ballina, peeling lino, a gas stove and white curtains but no black and white cat.

'This is great,' he says, 'it's like out of Lilliput. Everything is tiny.'

'You too,' she says.

'What's the rent?'

'Always, you ask me that. Since forever, what's the rent? The rent is my business. Tea or bed or both.'

'Bed then tea,' Tesky says, and Linda grabs his hand and drags him back down the hallway.

Tesky gets out of bed an hour later and walks back down the hallway to make a pot of tea. He sits down and smokes in the kitchen. Linda gave up. It seems impossible because whenever he thinks about her, she has a roll-your-own cigarette dangling from her lips. Not anymore, buster. He was looking forward to sitting up in bed and smoking while he drank the tea.

'Hey, Tesky, can you please smoke outside? It stinks, I can smell it already.'

He opens the back door and steps out. The cement is still warm on his feet. He touches a tree fern. Walks across the courtyard to the shed and opens it. Neatly stacked with gardening tools and a couple of fold-up chairs and a picnic table. The courtyard is spotless, and he thinks about Linda's room. No clothes on the floor. She used to just strip and leave the clothes where they fell for days, weeks on end. The big comfortable double bed. Must be new. He must check out the lounge room.

He steps back into the house but immediately feels like another smoke and he knows he's going to have to keep coming out here. Shit. He smokes one more cigarette and goes back to the bedroom.

'Do you have any mints? Maybe just clean your teeth. I can still smell those foul things.' Tesky gets up and cleans his teeth. Shit.

'What was your big news? What were you going to tell me?' Tesky takes a deep breath.

'I might do another course on making stained glass or a more advanced course. I might be able to get work doing it. You saw the ones I made, they were good.'

'Yeah, they were good, really good. Great, that's great Tesky. I have some news too.'

'Fire away.'

'I've started my own business making clothes. I have a woman who works for me, and I rented a small workplace in Ultimo. It's really going well. I keep getting more and more customers.'

'Ah, that's great, Linda, really good.' Tesky feels like he's been upstaged.

'And the big news, the really big news is that I might be buying this little house. I showed the bank my business plan and they can see I'm saving heaps of money and the guy who owns it wants to sell and then there's the first homeowners grants from the state and federal governments.'

Tesky thinks about sitting in the kitchen in Ballina: the free dope, the canning factory, the black and white cat, and about having sex with Sandra.

CIGARETTES

'This guy I used to go to uni with, Mick Costa, he rang me at work today.'

'And?'

'And he wants to visit me. I told him OK, but I haven't seen him for five or six years and he lives in Sydney now.'

'Randall, you told him he could stay here? Why? You've never spoken to me about this guy before and he's coming to visit. For how long?'

'Just a few days, that's what he said. He just broke up with his girlfriend and...'

'And he's at a loose end and he's going to want to re-live the great uni days with you while I die of boredom.'

'You want to know the truth? I never went out drinking with Mick, not a lot anyway. It's difficult to say. He went to the parties but with his girlfriend, always. Mick and I used to just talk about writers, films, books and art and politics. Religion. All those things you're not supposed to talk about in the pub.'

'You used to sit and talk...'

'Don't even say it. I know. I know. How could I have possibly been this other guy that I'm now telling you about?'

'I just can't see you in black jeans and a black turtleneck sweater with patches on the elbows, on the lawn at Melbourne Uni, talking earnestly about Dostoevsky with this guy, what's his name, Mick Costa?'

'You knew I went there for a year.'

'You never talk about it.'

'It was great, and you know I lived in Sydney for a year after that. Well, Mick Costa and his lover, Sophie, they were there at the time, not that I saw them all that much...but like I said, I did see them, they were at these parties but...I have to tell you about those two. Inseparable is not the word for their relationship...they were...hang on, how can I make you understand.'

'Just bloody tell me!' Madeline says.

And Randall runs his fingers through his thick mop of brown hair and smiles and says, 'OK. Mick Costa graduated from Melbourne University with a BA in 1992 and he and Sophie Lang moved to Sydney and lived in Leichardt because they'd heard it had this great café culture along Norton St and they didn't want to live in Glebe or Bondi or Newtown or Darlinghurst. Different. If there was one word to describe those two, it was different.'

'You're talking about them in the past tense.'

'Mick just rang me. This is what I'm telling you. It's hard to think of those two not together.'

'Tell me all about the golden couple,' Madeline says.

'They used to have coffee every morning, and I mean every morning, at Bar Italia in Norton St. I went with them a few times. Mick used to just give the Barista the money, the guy knew his order. Mick had a strong flat white and Sophie had a short black. And they sat outside and smoked their heads off and didn't talk to anyone but each other. They were in love, sure. It was more than that though. They found each other fascinating, the views they each held on everything from books to politics to religion and everything in-between. They went to parties together and sat down and talked to each other all night while the party went on around them. Mick and Sophie. The only place they weren't together were their part-time jobs. Mick worked in a service station in Annandale two nights a week and Sophie worked at Sappho Books in Glebe Monday to Wednesday, from midday to five.'

'Are they attractive, good-looking? What do they both look like?' Madeline asks.

'Sophie was, is, beautiful. Ethereal. Voluptuous. Dark hair and olive skin but she has blue eyes. Amazing sky-blue eyes. She didn't have dark brown skin but still those eyes, the contrast, and she talked like...like an old Hollywood actress, like Lauren Bacall but it wasn't ridiculous. Mick. Mick's a good-looking, strong, black curly-haired, Greek guy. Intense. He'll be here on Friday so...'

'So, yada yada, yada,' says Madeline but she's intrigued.

'I'm at the office. Mick's coming here at 5PM. We'll have a couple of beers in The Windsor—nothing but the best.'

'I'm going to order Thai when you get home, see you.'

Madeline kills a couple of hours making phone calls to her friends and trying to find just one who knew Mick Costa and Sophie Lang. Zero. They're untraceable except for her husband.

Randall opens the front door and Madeline goes to him, kisses him on the mouth with one eye on her guest. Randall puts his briefcase under the telephone table in the hall, turns to Mick and with a big smile on his face says, 'Madeline, Mick. Mick, Madeline.'

They shake hands and Madeline thinks he looks so much younger than she thought he would. Intense was what Randall said but beautiful is what Madeline thinks. Randall talked about Sophie's blue eyes, the contrast. But Mick, he's got these huge, almost black, eyes and his hair is wavy, not curly, a thick, strong body. He stands like a boxer or an athlete, loose, waiting to move.

And she says to him, 'I'm ordering Thai take-away. Do you have a preference?'

'Count me in. Just add one to whatever you're ordering for you two.'

And Randall and Mick move to the lounge and Randall says, 'Sit, sit,' to Mick, who gravitates to the oldest armchair in the room, the one covered with an old rug to hide the rips in the upholstery and it fits him like a glove. He's dressed in black Lee jeans, thick, hard black walking shoes, not Docs, something heavier in style, and a red shirt with the classic, slackers, black leather jacket, that sits tightly on his shoulders and finishes just below the waist. He lights a cigarette without asking and looks around for an ashtray and Madeline fetches one from the kitchen. Randall's wearing a brand new, off-the-rack, Oxford suit, with a very clean white shirt, MCC members tie and black brogues. They look at each other and don't know what to say. Five years, close to six. Mick still does a couple of nights at the Annandale service station and Randall makes over two hundred grand a year, not to mention Madeline's solicitor's salary.

Mick tells them he took Sophie's shifts at the bookshop when she quit and moved...back here...back to Melbourne somewhere. He looks at Randall and says, 'Fantastic house, Randall. Brilliant.'

'What are you doing, Mick?' he asks even though he's just been told. Madeline comes into the room.

'The same stuff I did when you were in Sydney. The servo and, I told you, I took Sophie's job at the bookshop when she left and it's difficult. I...'

'It's cool, mate,' Randall says and Madeline asks, 'How long do you plan on staying?'

'Just a couple of days. I have ten days off but I'm going to find a cheap motel in the city somewhere.' And no-one quite knows what to say. That awkward dead silence.

Madeline breaks it open with, 'I hear you and my husband use to be the campus intellectuals?' And they both look at each other and remember and laugh and they keep laughing for a few minutes.

Randall gets up and asks, 'Beer, Mick? I got three Coronas and as many Stella as you can drink.'

'I'll take a Corona.' And the night begins. Madeline wants in on this, the old stories and the story of Mick and Sophie from Mick.

'Do you remember Dale Watson?' Randall asks, and that's how it plays out for an hour or so, small talk about people they knew at Uni and in Sydney, but Madeline can see Mick's not really into it and maybe it's because of what Randall told her. Mick had his Sophie and that was enough for him. She can see he's all kind of repressed and tightly wound up, energy wanting to burn right out of his body but he can't lay it on Randall, he can't lay it on anyone. An hour goes by and Mick kind of eases back into his chair, nearly relaxing but tense still, and he's knocked back the three Coronas and Randall just brought him a Stella Artois and he lights another cigarette which is driving Madeline crazy but she can't bring herself to say anything.

In fact, he looks so wound up, she just has to ask him, 'Do you want to tell us more about what happened with you and Sophie? It might help to talk?'

And Mick's dumbfounded, twists in the chair and doesn't know where to look. Takes a big swig of his beer, looks down, drags on his cigarette. Takes a depth breath and says, 'Maybe later, huh.' And he may as well have said, mind your own fucking business.

Three days later Madeline calls Randall at work.

'Do you know where your friend Mick went to stay, which motel?'

'I thought you were glad to see him go, too morose, too serious for you.'

'The other half of your chosen two, Sophie Lang just rang. It seems your friend, Mick, was the one who did the runner. She's in Leichhardt wondering where the hell he is and thought as a long shot she might call you.'

'Mick left Sophie?'

'Yep.'

'Did you get her number?' Madeline gives him the number. She's working at home today. The whole thing has kind of thrown her. Mick was intense, brooding. The old cliché of the dark-haired, brooding, macho guy who says little or nothing and she found herself attracted to him. She doesn't know the guy, just giving life to some of her thoughts.

Randall looks at the phone number he wrote down. Sophie Lang. No-one had a chance. You didn't even bother trying. Firstly, because Mick would have killed anyone who went near her, and secondly, she was so obviously in love with him and here's the proof, she's trying to chase him down. Why would Mick lie though, and why would he leave her and make up all that stuff about taking her job?

He makes the call to her mobile phone and gets that Hollywood actress voice saying, 'Sophie would love to talk to you as soon as she gets a chance, please leave a message.' And Randall felt a stirring at the sound of her voice and left the following message, 'Soph, I got your message from my wife, please call me back.' And he left his own mobile number and wondered why he called her Soph; he never ever called her that before. Mick, Mick, which motel did you say you were going to stay in? You said you'd call me, but you told me the name of it, it... it's...shit!

Randall can't concentrate on his work. He's going crazy trying to remember the name of the motel and he's going crazy at the sound of Sophie Lang's voice in his brain. He gives up at 4.30PM. He normally works until 6PM at least.

Madeline can't concentrate either, she wants to know why Mick left the beautiful, ethereal, voluptuous Sophie Lang, who sounded to die for on the phone when she left her mobile number for Randall.

Randall gave Mick his number, but he didn't get his in return and Mick called him at work from Sydney when this whole thing started. So, he's pissed off when he reaches home and opens the front door and Madeline's all dressed up and about to go out.

'Where are you going?' he asks.

'I organised to go out with Sam and Alice. A girl's night, just dinner, no dancing. I haven't seen them for ages and...Did you call, Sophie? What did she say?'

'I only got her voicemail, and she hasn't called me back. I

can't remember where Mick said he was staying and I gave him my number but didn't get his.'

Madeline shrugs and kisses him on the lips. 'See you later on. Not late. Love you.' And she's gone.

Sophie calls Randall. 'Have you seen, Mick?' she asks him.

'Yeah, he stayed here on his first night and then moved to a motel in the city, but I don't know which one.'

'You're not protecting him are you, Randall?' she asks, and Randall just loves the sound of her voice saying his name.

'No, I'm waiting for him to call me. I have to tell you, Sophie, he told us, my wife and I, that you left him, he even said he took over your job at the bookshop.' And Randall feels instantly like an arsehole for putting his friend in the shit but he's talking to Sophie Lang again.

'I had an affair, Randall,' Sophie says.

Randall gets a mental image of that and he says, 'I...I'll tell him to call you, Soph, that's all I can do.' But he wants to keep her on the phone and he tries to think of something else but she just says, 'Alright,' and hangs up.

Madeline is at a small bar in Flinders Lane, in the city, talking with her friends. She told them about Mick Costa and they laughed and said, 'Ooh, where is he now?' And she felt protective of him and twenty minutes later she saw him, saw Mick Costa, slouched on a bar stool, drinking coffee and smoking. Then he got up to leave but changed his mind, sat back down and lit another one of those infernal cigarettes of his.

At 10PM she and her girlfriends decided to leave and she went with them but then cut back to the bar to see him sitting there, smoking, drinking coffee and brooding. She walks up and takes the vacant stool beside him.

He doesn't move, doesn't acknowledge her, so she says, 'You don't look happy, Mick.'

As he turns he starts to smile, which means he recognised her voice and he keeps smiling when he sees her blond hair and green-eyed looks. 'You're so different to Sophie,' he says.

'She called our house, Mick.'

'So, you know. You know I lied to you and Randall.' He exhales smoke as he says it and she likes it, likes the smell of him and cigarettes.

'Why did you make it up?'

'Sophie had an affair it seemed easier to lie.'

Mick walks out of the bar followed by Madeline and he stops at the front entrance and pushes a cigarette butt into the sand-filled ashtray. Madeline looks at him like he's a stray cat or something and says, 'Don't be a stranger, Mick. Come and see us. I...I don't know what to say.' Mick looks at her, touches her forearm and leans in and kisses her lightly on the lips and then leans back and smiles shyly. Madeline says, 'You shouldn't have done that.'

Mick sighs and brushes his hair back. Says nothing and they both look at the ground and then he says, 'I have to go.' He starts to walk off. Madeline says his name and he turns and says softly, 'I'm sorry. I shouldn't have done it.'

She watches him leave and says loudly, 'Mick!' He turns and comes back a few feet and Madeline says, 'What are you going to do now?'

'Kill myself.'

THE NEW BAR

J ulia sits in a bar in a little side street off Bayswater Rd, Kings Cross, Sydney. The bar opened three nights ago, and for some reason, they sent to her work (how did they know where I work?) an invitation to, 'join us for a drink'. The 'us' being the establishment itself and they threw in five free drink vouchers. She's on drink number three and it's 8.00PM and she's the only person, other than one staff member and a guy on his own collecting his free drinks as she is. He's sitting in the darkest corner of the bar and he's drinking Black Russians. When she walked into the bar, she felt a little odd, not déjà vu. More like a shift in time almost. Sounds stupid but like she had been transported, like Star Trek, when they used to step into the tubes and bingo, they ended up on Planet Nine or something.

The guy drinking Black Russians works as a barman at Springfields, a bar, curiously enough, in Springfield Lane in, yeah, Kings Cross. Springfields used to be the infamous Manzel Room. The Manzel had a reputation. A kind of 1970s or 1980s heroin chic, rock 'n' roll kind of gig. You went there to get, like Keith (you wish), elegantly wasted. If you were in Springfields, right now, in 1996, at 8.00PM. You'd be surrounded by small and large TV screens and the one-day cricket between Australia and Sri Lanka would be on screen. Steve Waugh would be on screen hitting a four off an off-spinner whose name escapes me. He looks like Patel, the Kiwi off-spinner. So, you wouldn't want to be there if you were out to get elegantly wasted. Times change, some of us don't.

Julia is a receptionist at the Hyatt. The Hyatt takes pride of place along with the huge Coke sign on William St, at the top of The Cross. Julia lives on her own in a 'studio apartment' on Macleay St. If studio apartment makes you think of a groovy New York Loft pad, you're out of your mind. It's a smallish room, double bed and sofa take up pretty much the whole room, small bathroom—standing room only for one person, a kitchen off the lounge with the basics, but she likes it. No, she *loves* it. If she stands on her tippy toes, she can see Sydney Harbour Bridge through the bathroom window. It's her state-ment to the world. She can hack it on her own. She can bring men home or not. She pays all the bills. She doesn't need a car. Everything is on her doorstep. She lives in a red-light, druggy, cosmopolitan, groovy, cool area in her little studio apartment and she loves it.

How come this place only invited her? What about Vicki, Sophie, Helen, and the other guys at work, why her? No reason. She was on a list compiled by a computer. She signed in at some drongo club in Randwick of all places, writing down where she worked, and bingo, free drinks. The other two guys she was with that night wrote down false names and one of them said he worked at 'Spacy's on the Beach', something he made up on the spot. The bar she is in right now, with the guy drinking Black Russians, is called The New Bar.

'I thought this was opening night,' she says to the barman. 'Where is everyone?'

'That was three days ago,' he says.

'So, why would you send me drinks vouchers for tonight when nothing's happening?'

'Because tonight is special,' he says.

'Oh.' And she looks over at the guy drinking Black Russians.

The guy drinking Black Russians is Andrew. So, we have Julia and Andrew. Some lights come on to reveal a small stage, way on the opposite side to where Andrew sits. Drum kit, guitars resting, low black lights at the front of the stage pointing to where the band should be.

'There's going to be a band, tonight,' she says to the barman.

'Yeah, The Band from Heaven, they call themselves.'

'Wow,' Julia says. 'The Band from Heaven.' The barman's name is Zendo, (what the hell sort of name is that, she thought) he's dressed in all black with a studded belt for show. Andrew comes to the bar.

'Last voucher,' he says to the barman, 'another Black Russian.'

Julia looks at Andrew and says, 'What's in a Black Russian?'

The barman answers, 'Vodka and Coke. Simple.'

Julia almost says, *I didn't ask you,* because he's a bit flaky in his cool black clothes and studded belt, but she smiles at Andrew instead. Andrew takes the drink and goes back into the darkness to sit on the soft, dark brown sofa in the corner of the bar.

Julia feels like she wants to ring someone, wants to tell them, 'The Band from Heaven are playing in this bar tonight,' but she doesn't. She wants to go and talk to the Black Russian guy. Low-wattage spotlights come on to light up a small circular dance floor in front of the stage. It's the smallest dance floor Julia's ever seen. Zendo smiles at her and she rubs her arms, and for a moment they feel like fish scales and she gets that shift in time feeling again. Planet Nine.

Zendo turns and walks out an exit at the back of the bar and Julia knows he's gone for the night. A beautiful young girl, she must be only just eighteen, walks in through the same exit and comes behind the bar. Julia's never seen anyone as beautiful as her in her whole life. She has long blonde hair down to her ass, in dreadlocks. Huge blue eyes and *'cheekbones like geometry'*, as Mr Lloyd Cole sang, still sings. Killer smile, her teeth aren't fake white, they're shiny clean natural white. She is stunning beyond belief and she tells Julia, 'Hi, my name is Nina.'Planet Nine. And she thinks, you know, I've never even seen this street before. The little street The New Bar is on. She doesn't want to leave though because The Band from Heaven will be playing and Andrew is walking to the bar to get his next and last Black Russian unless she can talk to him.

Music starts playing in The New Bar. Music like she's never heard before. Kind of trancy but with new wave sensibilities and maybe some Smiths influence she can detect. Julia doesn't know what she's on about and laughs to herself, but the music is hypnotic cool.

'What is this music?' she asks the young and beautiful Nina.

'The Number One Song in Heaven,' she says

Andrew hears her when he arrives at the bar and says to Julia and Nina, 'The Number One Song in Heaven, what an unusual name, but you have to like it, don't you?'

'Is it a band or what?' Julia asks. Nina shows her the record, yes, a record, not a CD. The cover is all white, back and front. In very small light (Sky) blue writing is written, 'The Number One Song in Heaven.'

'This is just unbelievable music, like a drug, I feel it moving inside me and around me, like I could fly almost,' Julia says. And Nina and Andrew don't laugh at her because they feel the same.

Andrew gets another Black Russian, and Nina says, 'It's on the house and whatever you'd like, Julia. On the house.' Julia didn't tell Nina her name and Andrew is sitting beside her on a bar stool now. 'The Number One Song in Heaven' is coursing through his veins and he could just stay in that spot forever, but the band are coming through a side door now, walking onto the stage, tuning the guitars, brushing the drums, the stage lights are still off.

'Planet Nine,' Julia says out loud.

'You too,' Andrew says and they both laugh. A big happy friendly laugh. No giggling. This is 'The Number One Song in Heaven', soon to be The Band from Heaven.'

No direction home.

ABOUT THE AUTHOR

 Sean O'Leary is a writer from Melbourne, Australia. He has published two literary short story collections, *My Town* and *Walking*. His literary novella *Drifting* was the winner of the 'The Great Novella Search 2016' and published in 2017. He self-published '*The Heat*', his crime novella set in Darwin and Bangkok in 2019. *Drifting* and *The Heat* will be republished by Next Chapter in the near future. His crime fiction collection *Wonderland* was recently published by the down-and-dirty folk at Close to the Bone Publishing in the UK. His crime novel *Going All the Way* and short story collection *Tokyo Jazz & Other Stories* have both been recently published by Next Chapter. He is currently working on the third instalment of the Carter Thompson series and ongoing short stories all the time.

He likes to walk all over the face of the earth, take photos like a madman, travel as often as he can, supports Melbourne Football Club (a life sentence), loves art, is crazy about films, and writes like a demon.

To learn more about Sean O'Leary and discover more Next Chapter authors, visit our website at www.nextchapter.pub.

This Is Not A Love Song
ISBN: 978-4-82415-538-2

Published by
Next Chapter
2-5-6 SANNO
SANNO BRIDGE
143-0023 Ota-Ku, Tokyo
+818035793528

2nd November 2022

Lightning Source UK Ltd.
Milton Keynes UK
UKHW012040090223
416722UK00003B/289